# THE BITTER EARTH

GRAHAM'S RESOLUTION, BOOK 5

A. R. SHAW

APOCALYPTIC VENTURES

ISBN: 9781980501169

ISBN 13: 9781980501169

Library of Congress Control Number: Pending

LCCN Imprint Name: Apocalyptic Ventures, LLC, Coeur d'Alene, Idaho

Publisher's Note: This is a work of fiction. Names, characters, places, and incidents are a product of the author's imagination. Locales and public names are sometimes used for atmospheric purposes. Any resemblance to actual people, living or dead, or to businesses, companies, events, institutions, or locales is completely coincidental.

Cover Designs by Hristo Argirov Kovatliev

Edited by Dr. Vonda of First Editing

*Dedicated to the fans of Graham's Resolution...at long last.*

# CONTENTS

# BOOKS BY A. R. SHAW

# 1

## LINCOLN

July 13<sup>th</sup>
Seattle, WA

A KNIFE LAY on the dewy grass before them. It was a neglected old blade by anyone's standards, somewhat misshapen, with a couple of small rust spots visible upon it. The black resin hilt was in no better condition. In a flash, the thief reached for it. Then, a low dangerous growl. In a firm voice, Officer Lincoln Asher said, "Touch it, and I'll release the K-9. Stop resisting. I don't want to hurt you."

The thief's shaking hand instantly retreated.

With one knee in the suspect's back, Lincoln gave Enzo a swift hand signal after he placed the handcuffs on the man's wrists. Then he rolled the prisoner onto his side and helped him sit up. Supporting him under the arm, he helped the prisoner into a standing position and dusted off the stray blades of grass clinging to the suspect's stained and torn gray t-shirt and baggy denim jeans.

Enzo came and sat directly in front of the man, continuously threatening him with the caveat of an attack; giving the thief the idea that at any instant he'd become the canine's lunch. That was the point. To keep the man wary so that Officer Asher could perform his job. That way, no one got hurt.

While Enzo kept the man busy, Lincoln drew out a plastic baggie and flipped it inside out to retrieve the knife on the ground. Enzo's growl intensified, which meant the man broke eye contact with the dog or that he'd moved his foot or dared to twitch a muscle. There were times Officer Asher thought that his partner might even hear the private thoughts of men and perhaps the guy would run for it.

No sooner had the premonition crossed Lincoln's mind that the guy might be that stupid, a flash of brown fur scrammed after him. Shaking his head at the audacity of some criminals thinking they could outrun a K-9, Officer Asher leisurely strolled over to where Enzo had quickly taken down the guy for a second time, jerking at his inner thigh while the man wailed, "Get him *off* me!"

"Trying to make things worse for yourself?"

"Ah, please. He's ripping my dick off!"

*If you run again, I'll let him,* thought Officer Asher and called Enzo off. "Stop resisting." Again, he helped the man up and this time, after checking the suspect's pockets and waistband for any other weapons, he walked him the three blocks back to his police car. Had he not run off in the first place, Lincoln would have gone easier on him, but after catching him trying to jimmy open the second-floor store window, he gave Asher no choice. He caught the robber in the act. On the way there, he radioed but "Suspect in cus..." was all he got out before the guy took off the first time.

After the chase and then the walk back, Officer Asher was breathing as hard as the suspect. The weather in the Seattle area rarely peaked over eighty degrees in the summer, but when it did the humidity made it feel like you were swimming in your own sweat. With his hand protecting the thief's bald, shaven head he helped him into the back seat of his patrol car, typically Officer Enzo's domain. Waves of heat poured off the man. The guy's face was filthy, with trails of sweat making clean rivers through the dirt on its way down. "Squad 6113."

The dispatch didn't answer right away. Lincoln looked at the mic as if perhaps he screwed up the call when dispatch answered after a delayed pause. "Go ahead, 6113."

"Squad 6113, I need a 10-16 for a male C-1...going to...D6," Lincoln said as he tried to catch his breath.

As he awaited a response, he eyed the prisoner. He wished he could offer him a bottle of water. He looked pretty rough. But procedures prevented the offering. Running on a day like this was hell on anyone, even thieves.

Though he wasn't supposed to engage in casual conversation he said, "Hot day, huh?"

The guy nodded and when he tried to reply, he coughed instead; a phlegmy congestion filled his mouth. He spit the thick wad to the side as Lincoln watched him, making sure he wasn't about to do something stupid. Then the prisoner sort of leaned against the squad car, letting all of his weight rest there.

Sweat began trickling down the sides of his face as he glanced up at the broiling sun overhead. Before he could respond, he noticed the prisoner sliding downward slowly. "Hey," he ordered. "Get out and stand, please." The prisoner continued his unconscious descent so that Officer Asher reached out and held him still by the shoulder.

The prisoner opened his eyes halfway then.

"I said, stand please," Lincoln warned him, though it seemed the prisoner was really out of it. Then he felt the waves of heat coming off the man through his grasp on his t-shirt. "Damn, you're hot. Are you ill?"

The prisoner nodded weakly and even that seemed to be a challenge.

"Squad 6113 to dispatch."

"Go ahead, 6113."

"Any word on my conveyance? And how about medical? My prisoner is starting to lose consciousness."

"Sorry 6113, the closest conveyance got called to a combative prisoner."

"What about medical?"

"Medical can...but we had to activate mutual aid. It's going to be at least thirty minutes."

He looked at the prisoner. *Damn...that's not going to work.* "6113 to dispatch, I don't think this guy has thirty minutes."

As if on cue the prisoner slumped slowly down to the side along the squad car to the ground.

Lincoln pulled him back up to a standing position, with his hands still handcuffed behind his back. Lincoln said, "Here..." He opened the back seat of the squad car. "Lie down." He helped him inside and shut the door after moving his legs inside.

"6113 to dispatch, I'm conveying my prisoner to Harborview Medical Center myself. I'm running out of options."

"10-4 on that, 6113; I will advise a supervisor to meet you at the hospital."

After that, Officer Asher looked down at Enzo and said, "Guess what buddy, you get to sit up front today."

Lincoln situated Enzo in the front passenger side of his unit and closed the door so that he could retrieve a few bottles of water from his cooler in the trunk. He twisted open one of them after setting the others on the roof of the car. He took in a deep breath and said, "Ah, hell with it." He opened the back door, where the prisoner briefly glanced at him before shutting his eyes again. "Here, have some water before we get going."

The man no less than guzzled down several large sips before he fell back into the seat shutting his eyes again. "Okay, I'm taking you to the hospital first."

The prisoner nodded, only this time he didn't even try to open his eyes.

Then it was Enzo's turn, knowing there would be little time to give the dog water while he stayed with the prisoner in the hospital until he was relieved by another officer.

"Hey, great job, partner," he said and poured water into a bowl and sat it down for Enzo to drink. Patting the dog and rubbing his fur vigorously, Lincoln wished he could remove the fur coat for the dog, perhaps with a zipper, to make him cooler in the warmer months. Though Enzo didn't seem to complain about the heat, Lincoln thought it had to be uncomfortable to wear a fur coat in such warm humid temperatures. Damp heat had a way of getting to the best of men. And to Lincoln, Enzo *was* the best of men.

Opening his own bottle of water finally, Lincoln tilted his head back and let the cool liquid quench his languishing thirst. The paperwork, or reporting as they called it now, would wait until after Lincoln conveyed the prisoner to the hospital. So much for protocol. Seemed everyone was making do with limited resources today.

After rolling down the windows of the car to keep cool while he cranked on the air conditioner, Lincoln felt heat swath over to the front seat in a hot, wet breeze. He found the air too stifling to sit inside with the excessive heat emanating off the suspect and his partner's panting making conditions worse. Finally feeling cool air coming out of the vents, he closed the windows and drove the few blocks to the hospital.

He wasn't sure what it was about the hot, muggy weather some were calling an Indian summer, but it was making the general population crazy-stupid. Every call he'd gone on the last few days, people were at each other's throats. They'd had more domestic violence calls than in recent history. One thing was for sure, since they lived in the Northwest, few homes had air conditioning and on the rare year when they needed it, violence rose with the temperatures at a fever pitch.

Lincoln never relaxed with a prisoner in custody. Having a K-9 unit, it wasn't customary to transport one anywhere. He constantly checked his rear-view mirror in case the guy somehow slipped his cuffs and pulled a weapon—a constant threat. He even watched him on the MDC, (Mobile Data Computer).

"How you doing back there?" Officer Asher asked, but there was no response from the guy secured in the back seat. With his eyes flashing back in the rear-view mirror, Lincoln watched as sweat dripped off the guy's jaw, running down the inside of his neck. He remembered having his hand on the man's head briefly to keep him from banging it on the roof, and when he did, it felt like an oven. Even with the outside heat the prisoner was emanating his own furnace.

"Dayum," Lincoln murmured to himself, knowing with the nip from Enzo and the fever, he and his partner were in for an investigation when the dust settled from this day. Usually, in case of a bite from a K-9 officer, a Sergeant was sent immediately to the scene due to *use of force*.

"This is going to take all day," he said to his partner riding shotgun as they made their way to Harborview Medical Center. Enzo's brown, soulful eyes met his. Reaching over, Lincoln scratched the dog under his police badge collar.

After losing his last K-9 during a home invasion call and subsequent firefight, Officer Asher didn't think he could take on another K-9 again. The pain of losing Khan was too much. He'd loved that dog as if he were his own brother and stayed with him in the emergency vet hospital, stroking his fur and talking to him all night as he fought for his life. Eventually, the bullets that entered his body took his life. The feeling of sheer anger made him want to shred the assailant by himself, no weapons necessary; he could do what was necessary with his bare hands if only they'd let him. Lincoln Asher was a calm man by most standards but not then...then, he was a madman capable of the most heinous murder.

After a few weeks, they brought Enzo to meet him. Neither of them wanted anything to do with each other at first.

Then his Captain said, "Linc, give him some time. He's just like you."

It seemed both man and dog were mourning the loss of their latest partners and time was all they needed to shed the grief. Enzo too had lost his previous officer to a bad day on the job. The ones, if you lived through them, you never forget and if you don't, the date becomes etched on your tombstone. No other private sector job was like that on a daily basis. You didn't go to work as a cashier, banker or tech support and risk your life every day. Of course, there were exceptional days when a criminal walked into those businesses with a killing intent, but for the most part they didn't put on a uniform and head into trouble like police officers did. Yet Officer Asher chose this job after his stint in the military. It's what he knew how to do and he was good at it. As it turned out, Enzo was good at it too and they'd turned out to be a great team.

The first night that Enzo came home with him, he felt like he was betraying Khan in a way by letting Enzo sleep on his bed, play with his toys and piss in the same spot that Khan had done before. In time, Lincoln got over what felt like an intrusion and instead he and Enzo became more than partners; they'd become friends.

Not long after, he and Enzo were a team like none other. It was as if the dog read his mind. Enzo operated by hand signals unlike any other canines that Lincoln had worked with before. They became so in tune with one another that Enzo would act just on eye contact.

Once they pulled up in front of Harborview Medical center, Officer Asher parked near the entrance and blasted the air conditioner on high again so that Enzo remained comfortable inside the vehicle while he escorted the sick man inside. When the suspect awoke perspiration poured off his forehead and his eyes were wild.

"Where are we?" He looked around as if he had no idea.

"The hospital. Come on, let's get you looked at. Can you walk?"

"What?"

"Can you walk on your own?"

"Yeah," he said, but Lincoln doubted those words.

"Okay, just a second," he said as he poured Enzo another bowl of water, sitting it in the back seat floor board, and moving Enzo to his regular area of the car. "Here you go, buddy. I'll be back as soon as I can." But when he pulled the man to a standing position, his knees buckled underneath him. "Whoa there, come on," he said, hoisting the skinny guy up by the arms.

Department SOP (standard operating procedure) dictated that he leave Enzo in the running locked car while he brought the suspect inside for medical treatment. If it was going to be for more than fifteen minutes he'd call for someone else to take over babysitting the suspect. And, by the looks of the overflowing parking lot, and the size of the crowd in the waiting room, he went ahead and called for another officer while he waited in line.

People coughed and wheezed like in a tuberculosis ward. Mothers paced the floor with feverish children lying over their shoulders. An old man came in complaining of chest pains and collapsed while waiting in line for a nurse to evaluate him. Ten minutes later he and the suspect had barely progressed inside the doorway.

Officer Asher was inclined to handcuff the guy to a gurney and leave him with the staff to get out of there since he was barely responsive, but he had to stay with him at all times. He was practically asleep leaning against him again. *God, you smell.* Obviously, he hadn't bathed in more than a day and with this heat, he reeked of body odor.

When a passing nurse glanced back at him and his uniform as she cut through the line, he held her up. "Nurse, how long is the wait? I've got a prisoner here who has a K-9 bite and he's running a fever. He's a flight risk so I can't just leave him here."

She looked him up and down like he was crazy, then she seemed to take pity on him. "I'll be honest, sweetheart, he won't see an actual doctor for like six hours, but I can move you forward since you're an officer of the law." She lowered her voice then and tugged on his sleeve to follow her. In a whisper, she said as she walked, "If I were you. I'd let him go and get out of here. Now. We're dealing with some crazy virus."

"I wish I could but that's not happening. I've got a K-9 waiting in the car. I can't leave him out there for long. Someone is supposed to take over for me here, but I don't know when they'll arrive. You mentioned a virus? I haven't heard anything about a virus."

Without answering his question, she led them through the line while several others flashed dirty looks his way but one look at his uniform and they held their tongues. He knew it wasn't fair but he had a job to do. The nurse led them to a little room with an exam table and two chairs. "You can wait here. I'll see if I can get someone as soon as possible since your partner is waiting in the car. Is he okay out there?"

"Yeah, he's fine but I might need to check on him in a few minutes. The air conditioner is going full blast and the engine's running."

"That's good. This heat is too much even for the dogs," she said and closed the door.

The suspect was nearly dead weight against his side. "Here, lie down," he said and helped the man up onto the papered examination table. Uncuffing one of his arms, he let the guy lie down flat on the gurney, the paper cracking with depression, and then Officer Asher cuffed one of the prisoner's arms to the side railing. He wouldn't be going anywhere, at least, not in his condition and certainly not handcuffed to the bed. When Officer Asher saw the nearby sink, he immediately washed his hands as well as possible. He'd learned long ago to do so while singing "Happy Birthday" to himself twice...seemed silly but now it was a habit. If the guy had the virus that the nurse mentioned, he certainly didn't want to risk contracting it and then giving it to Paige.

Thinking of her, he went ahead and called but only received her voice mail. "Hey, it's me. Listen, I might be a little late coming home. Don't wait up and please avoid any public places if you can; there's a nasty virus going around. I'm at the hospital right now with a suspect and everyone here is sick. I'll see you soon. Love you, bye."

As he began to put his phone away it buzzed in his hand. He thought it was her returning his call already, though when he looked, there was a message from Officer Gance. He was there to take over for him. "Whew!" he said and glanced at the sick man on the gurney. From what he could tell he was out cold. *At least I don't have to wait around for you, after all,* he thought as he texted his location back to the officer trying to find them in the labyrinth of an emergency ward.

When Officer Gance walked through the doorway, he wasn't smiling, nor did he seem the least bit happy to be there. He was an older man with graying hair, and no one would ever accuse him of holding too much compassion for his fellow man. Gance was known as a straight-forward guy, if not a little brutal in his delivery.

"Hey, at least it's air conditioned."

"Yeah, with germs," Gance said.

Lincoln laughed, "You'll be out of here in no time. He has a bite, courtesy of Enzo, on his right inner thigh. He's also running a pretty high temperature. The rest is on file. Thanks. I hate leaving Enzo in the car, especially in this heat, even though the air conditioner is running."

"Yeah, even though there's big lettering saying Keep Back on your unit, they're still hovering. I'm surprised you conveyed him yourself."

"I had no choice. No one was coming."

"It's a little crazy out there today. I saw Officer Enzo on the way in. He's doing fine, but there's a crowd filed out the waiting room doors and they're gawking at him."

"Great, I better get out of here then. Hey, thanks man. I owe you one."

"You sure do. Later, Asher," Gance said as Lincoln left.

Outside of the little exam room, Lincoln was shocked to see that the crowd seemed to have doubled during his time in the waiting room, if that were possible. Whatever the virus was it was coming on fast. Holding his breath for as long as he could, Lincoln tried to get through the crowd and out to his car as fast as possible. When he did exit the building's double sliding doors the hot, humid air nearly knocked him over. Then to find people gathered around his running car, which was creating more heat, was unsettling. "Excuse me. Make way, please," he said multiple times to get through the thick crowd. It wasn't that they were gathering there to get a look at Enzo; the squad car was actually just in the way of the building's emergency room door.

Finally, he was able to get inside of his squad car. After briefly checking on Enzo, who was panting but doing fine otherwise, he pulled out the hand sanitizer and slathered it between his palms and then took out a sanitizing wipe and swiped every surface he touched upon entering the squad car. Then he took off away from the hospital as fast as he could, dodging between the growing crowd. It was the end of his shift and since he was able to drive directly home due to having a K-9 unit car, he headed straight there through the increasing traffic.

## 2

## WONG

Beijing, China

Now, without a sound, the snowflakes drifted down past the spent cherry blossoms, piling higher against a black leather shoe, freezing the shoelaces into oblong moons hanging by a thread. Fan Wong watched as a white flake melted against the hard black leather, turning from its crystallized form into its liquid form once again with the aid of the body heat from the person sitting next to him on the frigid bench. A process he couldn't help but admire.

Sliding his glasses up the short bridge of his nose once again, he reminded himself to listen to the conversation. This was not the time to zone out as he was prone to do.

"...and your sister will return to you when you make the exchange. Do you have any questions?" They spoke in English so that others in the park would not readily overhear their very secret conversation. His tone was clipped with an accent. The speaker, an

Arabic man in his late forties, appeared scholarly and not out of place on a science campus.

Looking straight ahead, at the frozen pond, Fan Wong had no questions. Knowing what these people wanted meant only one thing...ultimately his death, their death, everyone's deaths.

In exchange for the virus he had developed, they would free his family. Only a temporary reprieve from the terror he knew would come soon after. When he completed this exchange, he would die as a traitor to his country, though few would really know this. If he didn't comply with the terrorists' terms, he would die at the hands of the terrorists, along with his family. There really wasn't a choice in the matter.

At only nineteen, Fan Wong was a prodigy. Hardly anyone even knew of his existence. He was a state secret, an asset to his country, but even so, once he made the exchange he was done for, as if his life meant nothing at all. The uniqueness that made him who he was and provided his family with the best living conditions amongst a society near poverty also came with its quirks. Fan Wong wasn't what anyone would describe as socially active. He was a loner, preferring the company of computer simulations and occasional video games over people any day. His mind was always churning with new ideas and mathematic solutions to problems society wasn't even aware of yet. The result of this was Fan Wong had no friends. Even the brightest among students shied away from him. He lived most of his life inward...within himself.

Just to cement the deal, the man sitting next to him on the bench passed him an iPad with a video on the screen. When he pressed the arrow, the video began to play. The image of his younger sister, age sixteen, came into view, her eyes frightened, her mouth gagged with a white cloth. A knife played over her tender jawline. Tears sprang to her eyes. She pulled away from the blade. Fan Wong tossed the iPad back to its owner. He stood. He bowed out of tradition and left, leaving his footprints in the snow across the once green lawn.

They'd contacted him easily enough by tapping into his computer. They'd sent messages at first, that he'd ignored. As a genius, Fan Wong wasn't easily influenced. As a socially awkward person, there wasn't a lot for them to use against him. He'd never used drugs and as for company with a partner, he preferred girls but rarely took the time to figure them out. It wasn't in his nature to spend time with others. Instead, his work at the virology institute was where he spent all of his time. What they were after was a controversial experiment, one that had already been done in America by a Chinese scientist who recreated the 1918 flu virus in a lab in the state of Wisconsin. The scientific community was outraged by the breach of ethics.

Fan Wong simply expounded on that discovery. Once the virus was genomed by the notorious scientist, the Chinese government obtained a sample. How, he did not know and didn't ask. He only improved the virility from 30% to 90%. Fan Wong understood the implications but was assured of anonymity, and his government needed the virus as a golden rod against the West if they ever needed such a weapon. Questioning authority was to dishonor his teachers and those that had educated him. So, though he worried about the implications, he did not confront his superiors.

As it turned out, his government heard the unsaid global warning, but nonetheless they'd used him to make the ultimate deadly weapon and now Fan Wong was in jeopardy because somehow the Islamic terrorists had found him and his creation. They had taken his family prisoner as the only leverage they had against him, and his life would never be the same. His own government would execute him if he complied with the terrorist. His family would die if he did not. They would all likely die if the virus was set free, which was something that Fan Wong expected to happen whether he helped them or not. These men had no morals when it came to humanity—a history well known.

# 3

## CLARISSE

The next morning, a graceful dawn peeked between the curtains, the bluish light ray falling over a form in a queen-size bed. Stirring as the beam of light widened over her closed eyelid, she twisted in the sheets, rolling from her side to her back in a sleepy attempt to escape the dawn.

Then the alarm sounded and her right arm swung around automatically and slapped the annoyance. Back on her side again, Clarisse pushed herself up into a sitting position, still with clenched eyes, not willing to face the day. "Come on, get up," she said, willing herself awake.

The long nights were catching up with her. Near the alarm clock, her hand felt around for her glasses. Putting them on her face in an automatic gesture, she still fought the urge to open her eyes, even though she might be able to see more than mere shadows now with her lenses on. Standing by pure will, only her body was functioning, her thought process still needing the snooze time allowed. Clarisse stood in her white tank top and underwear and reached for her dresser. She'd discarded the plaid flannel pants sometime during the night when her legs felt too hot. Her long chestnut hair cascaded down her back in a tangled mass.

After retrieving a pair of cotton underwear from her dresser drawer, she went into her bathroom, removed her nightshirt and showered. Letting lukewarm water cascade over her sleepy body, she started to waken. Seven minutes later, she was through bathing and stepped out, eyes wide open; somewhere between the alarm and the water her brain was fully functioning. She blamed her morning grogginess on low blood pressure. Though it meant she was calm, cool and collected most of the time, it also meant she had a hard time waking fully first thing in the morning.

Stepping out, she dried off and then stood on the scale, then remembered she couldn't see the numbers without her glasses and put them on again. At 127 pounds, she vowed not to skip lunch like she was prone to do during her busy days at work, knowing that when she dipped below that threshold she easily became anemic and she couldn't afford health problems with the hectic work schedule she currently kept.

"Great, another lunch avoiding Hector." It didn't matter how she gave him the brush-off, the guy just didn't get it. She'd contemplated filing a report with HR, but in her experience those things never worked. Handling the guy herself wasn't working much either, but she had no choice really. She had to keep a low profile. Making waves in the company that fed her wasn't a good idea, not with the knowledge she had, knowledge that could break a man—or a woman, in this case. Yet she bore the implications well.

Though the Virology Center of the Northwest was in plain sight, it was what she in particular was doing that wasn't common knowledge. Not even her superiors were privy to the studies she was conducting for the government.

Her past military experience and subsequent security clearance was the only reason they'd contacted her for the top-secret experiments having to do with a weaponized form of bird flu unlike anything that had ever been found, even the infamous so-called Spanish flu of 1918. A secret vial was now in her secure refrigerated lab with only a number as an ID for the treacherous makings inside the container.

It was why she'd lost so much weight in the past few weeks and why sleep came to her late and she couldn't shake off the burden easily in the morning. What she did during the day was the saving of plagues. The kind that wiped out all of mankind. Clarisse was careful, the problem was making such a thing to combat something so dreadful wasn't as easy as making the plague to begin with. That was easy...stopping death was more daunting than creating death, much more daunting.

She'd been at the forefront of stopping the ease with which scientists played around with such things of destructive properties, a mistake she was sure would happen all too easily. *A global disaster in the making*...was the phrase that kept running through her mind. Her job was to find a vaccine for such disasters before they became a viral menace and lately she was having a hard time keeping up.

Just as Clarisse managed to put her hair up into her usual bun, her spare phone buzzed. She pressed a bobby pin into place and had the last one still between her lips. "Dah, just a second." This phone was the one she kept with her at all times next to her main phone. She kept it charged and rarely did it make a sound, but when it did, she spared no time in answering the message. "Code 2" was what she read.

Her jaw dropped slightly. She scooped the phones up, grabbed her leather tote that she kept the latest journals and work that she could bring home with her in and headed for the entrance, swiping her keys off the side table on her way out the door of her small Seattle apartment.

# 4

## LINCOLN

At the same time across town, Enzo nosed Lincoln as he lay in bed, not yet ready to meet the day. When he didn't move, Enzo slid his wet nose against Lincoln's cheek. Lincoln turned over, laying a hand on Enzo's neck when he did. He scratched the dog around the scruff and underneath the collar but he hadn't yet moved himself. Enzo began licking his arm.

"Dude...love you, too. Gimme a sec. I swear, I'm up."

When he went still and silent for a time, Enzo licked his face this time, right across his parted dry lips. "Okay, I'm up. I'm up."

As he swung his feet to the bare floor, he rubbed his eyes and looked at Enzo panting beside him, his brown eyes adoring. "You're a weirdo sometimes, aren't you?"

Enzo seemed to smile as he looked at Lincoln and headed for the door, looking back at him.

"I'm coming, I'm coming," Lincoln said, knowing Enzo needed to go outside. He followed the dog to the backdoor slider and looked out before opening. Seeing no one careless enough to stray into his fenced backyard, Lincoln opened the slider and Enzo slipped outside. That's when he smelled coffee. "Paige, thank God. You're a saint," he said and found her in the kitchen sipping a cup, her blonde hair a wild mass of long curls. "Why didn't you let Enzo out?"

"He didn't come to me," she said.

"Hmmm, did you stay out late last night?" he said as he poured himself a cup of black brew and leaned against the kitchen counter, crossing his hairy bare feet and trying not to make it look like an inquisition.

"What if I did? None of your business, brother."

"Paige, it *is* my business."

"Just because you're a cop and my older brother, that doesn't mean you get to boss me around."

He was so tired of her pulling the little sister thing. She was an adult now. "Look you're twenty-five years old. I'm not treating you like a child. I'm treating you like my sister. Someone I care about. I'm just interested in how you're doing. Look, I just want you to be safe."

"Then stop trying to pry into my life, Linc," Paige said and slipped by him through the galley kitchen and into her bedroom.

"Hmm..." Lincoln sighed as she left. He never knew how to handle his little sister but that didn't matter now because Enzo stood outside the glass door waiting to be let inside. "All done, buddy? Ready to get to work? Then let's go."

Once he and Enzo were ready to leave, Lincoln called out to Paige, who had her music up in her room. "Paige, I'm headed out. I'll see you tonight. All right? Paige!"

"All right!" she yelled from her bedroom. "Don't yell at me!"

"Geez," he said, rolling his eyes. He couldn't help but think of his sister and their less than ideal situation on his way into work. After his father died, his mother couldn't handle Paige on her own. She was dealing with the severe effects of multiple sclerosis at the stage that she wasn't expected to live another year, and she didn't. Paige was only eighteen then. So he took his sister in right after he was discharged from the military, even though he was still only a kid himself.

She was a handful from the start. It was as if his sister was angry at the world and found only him to blame, though he had nothing to do with her existence. He loved her and did what his father would have expected of him. She'd made it through school fine and was getting through college but her attitude toward him never seemed to improve. He was her authority figure and a cop, which didn't seem to make the situation any easier. He just wished she didn't sneer at him every time he came home. A smile or two every now and then was all he'd asked for. A little appreciation for what he'd done for her was, of course, too much to ask, but then again, expecting that of her was a futile effort.

He suspected Paige felt the world owed *her*, not the other way around. Complaining was an art form to his little sister. Smiling to himself at her audacity, he shook his head a little as he drove into the station. Catching a glimpse of Enzo in the back seat. "You ready for the day, buddy?"

Enzo's smiling eyes looked directly at him through the rearview mirror. That was his answer. Enzo was ready and so was he. They pulled into the station and checked in for the morning briefing. Attendance in the room was nearly half; seemed several officers were sick at home with the same flu. It was going to be another long day. He didn't complain though, just took care of business and got going. Once Enzo was seated in the back, they headed out.

The briefing he'd received once he hit the station was more of the same in escalation from the warm temps. The guy he brought into the hospital the day before was apparently still very sick. They admitted him. It seemed what ailed him had nothing to do with the dog bite but rather the fever he was running before then, and it had become much worse. He'd asked if he needed to go and babysit him but the doctors had put him in isolation and he remained handcuffed to the bed with an officer on watch. He wasn't going anywhere and since they needed all the officers they could get, the decision was made to postpone the investigation into the use of force until things got back to normal. It was simple...they needed him to work. They were even short of supervisors to perform the investigation itself.

"Things are nuts," Lincoln said as he thought about the situation.

Then his radio informed him of an incoming call. "Go ahead, dispatch."

"6113, we got a call again from your favorite troublemaker. You're the only one who can handle him. Do you mind? I know it's not your area today."

Linc took in a deep breath. Already, he'd have to deal *him* today. "Yeah...I'm on my way," he said as he ran a frustrated hand through his hair.

"Enzo, you ready? Time to babysit our old buddy."

Heading east to Highway 90, they exited left over the highway and pulled up to a little house just beside a gas station. If asked, Officer Asher couldn't tell you how many times he'd made this same call in the past few years. As long as the guy wasn't a threat to himself or anyone else, the procedure was to leave him alone but that wasn't always the case. Horacio Campos was a medicated man and some-times he forgot to take those meds, and when that happened all hell broke loose in his neighborhood. If he stayed on the meds, he was... almost a functioning member of society.

Campos had never been known to harm others, but he sure scared the crap out of many with the way his demeanor often changed on a dime; he seemed to suddenly switch personalities and some of them were so frightening, they were downright evil. Ulti-mately, he'd noticed Horacio was a nice fellow, when he was *himself,* but his alter egos were anything but. In his research of the case, that was usually the norm with those suffering with schizophrenia.

That, and Enzo often emitted a low growl whenever he was within a short distance of Campos. He just didn't seem to like the guy at all and if Enzo didn't like him, Lincoln didn't either. It was a main-tenance call. One they made at least once every few weeks it seemed now. Either the man's father, and only guardian, needed to admit him into some kind of care facility or they needed to tweak his meds because what he was taking now wasn't working and the old man was in his twilight years. He didn't have much time left. Some changes needed to be made and made soon.

Pulling into the driveway, Officer Asher looked around first. There was a small crowd of customers forming near the little store entrance at the gas station that the father owned and operated. "Looks like trouble," Asher said as he pulled in and stopped. A few of the folks in the crowd saw him coming, lowered their eyes to the ground and walked away, whereas Campos Senior and a woman continued their conversation in earnest. "Looks like that is getting a little heated," Lincoln said to Enzo.

As soon as he stepped out of the unit, loud voices were raised. Assessing the situation, Lincoln noticed Campos Junior was not anywhere in view. He walked over to the group of five people arguing with the owner. "What's going on here?" he asked cautiously.

A large woman with short blonde hair wearing black capris and a tank top two sizes too small faced him, tears in her eyes. "His employee came up behind me and yelled at me. Said I wasn't wanted here while I was pumping gas."

"That's because you threw your trash out of your big ass van and trashed the place, lady. You didn't even bother to put it in the cans. My son is sensitive to littering."

The middle-aged woman's face flooded red and she turned on her heel back to the old man. "He's your son? He's dangerous. That man's crazy!"

"Mr. Campos, where is your son right now?"

"He's in the house. She upset him. Was screaming at the top of her lungs at him."

"Ma'am, can I ask you a couple of questions, please?"

"You should be asking him the questions."

Nodding, he replied, "I will but your statement first." He led her over to the side of the building. "Tell me exactly what happened," he said as he pulled out his notepad.

Shaking, with tears streaming down her puffy cheeks, she said, "I was cleaning out my van while pumping gas. Some of the trash fell out onto the ground, that's true. Before I could pick it up, that man's son ran out and started yelling at me. At the top of his lungs he screamed at me."

"Name?"

"Suzanne Flynt."

"Did he touch you in any way?"

She shook her head, "No."

"Did he call you any insulting names?"

"Um, no. But he *scared* me," she said and broke down, fat tears flowing down her cheeks. She seemed to shake at the recent memory. "I thought he was going to attack me."

"What's your date of birth?"

Her eyes daggered at him as she spat out, "March 26, 1958."

He didn't care about her annoyed tone. "Driver's license, please," he asked and held out his hand while she rummaged through her purse.

Pulling it out she handed it to him with a thump into his palm. He didn't really need the driver's license. He could just look up the information with her name, but what the hell?

"Is everything current?"

"Yes!" she spat.

He gave her a warning look.

She blinked.

"Did he touch you? Threaten you in any way?"

"No, but he had this wild look in his eyes like he was going to. Can't you do something about him? I've seen him here before. He's dangerous."

Understanding her concern as a human being, he could only offer her this advice. "Ms. Flynt, if you were concerned for your safety knowing he worked here, why didn't you just leave? There are plenty of gas stations around."

"I...I don't know," she said. "It's a free country. Why can't I use this one?"

He shook his head. "Do you have any other information to add to this statement?"

Wiping the snot from her nose she said, "No! You're not going to do your job, are you? He should be arrested. That man shouldn't be out in public. He could hurt someone."

Though he didn't disagree with her, there wasn't much he could do until Campos did harm someone. Yelling at someone to pick up their trash wasn't a crime. His eyes flashed to her van, still parked near the pump. "Is that your van?"

"Yes," she said as he walked over to the older blue monstrosity. She followed behind him, each step a test of her swollen ankle joints.

Trash spilled out of the trashcan, some of it caught in the automatic closing lid. Greasy fast food wrappers littered the ground around the receptacle. Peering into the van, he could see there was a plethora of food wrappers still inside, littering the floorboard and passenger side and caught between the closed door. Not one but two big gulp containers were still transfixed to her cup holder in the center console...the ones that extend beyond the vestibule.

The other trashcans lining the gas station pumps were all completely tidy, no trash in sight.

"Ms. Flynt," he pointed at the trash on the ground, "does this belong to you, too?"

Watching her face pale, he thought for sure she was going to say no at first, but certainly she was thinking through her options. Finally coming to a conclusion, she said, "Yes."

With his pencil, he made a note of the situation on his pad of paper and then called in her plate number to dispatch. "Please stay right here," he said as he went back to the father with two other people standing beside him.

"Mr. Campos, did you see what took place here today?"

"I didn't but this man did." He motioned next to him to a guy wearing a plaid shirt, jeans and a trucker's cap.

"Your name?"

"Jeff Guthrie."

"Contact number?"

"509-228-0479."

"Mr. Guthrie, did you see what took place here?"

"I'm a truck driver." He pointed to the semi parked alongside the station. "I was eating my lunch when I saw that blue van pull up. That woman got out and started pumping gas and then she started shoving armloads of trash into the can there. I mean armloads." He held his arms out wide in front of him in a large semi-circle. "The whole time she was pumping gas, she kept going back for more and more. The mailman came by and pointed her out to Mr. Campos' son. There was trash all over the place and she didn't seem to care at all that it was flyin' all over. Like nothin' I ever seen before. I mean, I eat as much fast food as the next guy but jeez. Throw your damn trash away. I don't blame him for yellin' at the woman. She didn't give a damn that she was littering up the place. Walked around like she owned the station. I know Campos and his father. He can be a little odd at times but that woman's a slob."

"But did you see him verbally assault her?"

"Officer, I saw what any man would do. He yelled at her to clean up her mess. I mean look at that. I know Campos has problems but sir, this wasn't his fault. If anyone ought to get a citation it ought to be her. And she was yelling at him, too."

"She was?"

"Yeah, she got right in his face. Spitting at him, even. I'm surprised he didn't lose it. I would've. And Campos didn't do anything other than yell at her. Never touched her. After a while, she wasn't going to do anything and I saw him smile really weird at her. Then his dad here came out and told him to go inside."

"Did he comply willingly?"

The trucker thought about it. "Senior Campos had to say it more than once but he did comply. Campos turned and headed to their house."

"Okay, thanks," he said and then approached Campos Senior. "Do you think your son is a danger to himself or others?"

"No," Mr. Campos said, but Officer Asher doubted the conviction in his voice.

"Where's your son right now?" The old man's eyes were drawn down. He seemed defeated. With his arm, he pointed to the house and barely audibly he said, "He's inside, like usual."

"Why don't you come with me for a second and we'll go see how he's doing."

Passing his patrol car, Officer Asher visually checked on Enzo before going into the house. Campos Senior led the way and when inside they found Horacio sitting at the kitchen table drinking a glass of water. The house very was tidy for two bachelors; there was no way his house ever looked this neat.

"Horacio, Officer Asher would like to ask you a few questions."

The nearly black eyes looked up at him. It was the sneer on his face that sent an ominous twinge up his spine. "Hi there, Mr. Campos. Can I ask you a few questions?"

With a quick shiver of his head as if he were trying to shake off confusion, Campos looked up at him again, this time with a different look in his eyes. One of recognition.

With still no answer to his question, he tried repeating it. "Can I ask you a few questions, Horacio? You remember me, right? I was here a week or two ago...about the incident with the stray dog? Before that it was something else."

He nodded.

"The lady out front, the one with the blue van. Can you tell me what happened out there?"

"I... ah," he wiped his face and shook his head. "I remember Jeff coming inside to tell me she was littering. I looked out there and saw trash; garbage was everywhere. Greasy hamburger wrappers were drifting out from under her van. Those things...if you leave them out, they attract bugs, you know? Worms will grow wherever they land and the ants..." he said, shivering with disgust.

"Yeah, I've seen that happen. What happened next?"

"I...I don't know. Did she clean it up?" he asked with concerned eyes, looking up at him. If Lincoln didn't know better, he would have thought the man hadn't been there for the yelling himself. His eyes were as innocent as any he'd ever seen.

"You don't remember confronting the lady and asking her to clean up the mess?"

He looked to his father. "I didn't. I don't think so. Did I, Dad?"

His words were so convincing, Officer Asher looked to the father for an explanation as well.

Senior Campos didn't reply to his son; instead, he looked to

Lincoln. "My son sometimes doesn't remember things sometimes. Things he's done or said."

"Okay, yeah, I remember that about him...so, Campos, how did you get back in the house? What do you remember after seeing the lady's trash all over?"

He stared off into space. "I...came to the house. I think. Did you tell me to come to the house, Dad?" he asked his father.

Senior Campos nodded solemnly. "I did."

Watching the exchange, Officer Asher knew there was more to the story about Campos' condition that might explain the situation. "Um, Mr. Campos," he addressed the senior, "can I have a word?"

"Sure," he said and motioned for him to step back outside.

They moved to the front of the squad car. "Is he taking his medication?"

The old man's rheumy blue eyes looked into his as he took a deep breath and let it out. "He is, but they don't seem to be working well enough. I'll get him back in to the doctors soon. I think he might be skipping them every now and then."

"Well, for his sake and yours, I think you need to get on that. Get him in to be evaluated again, please. We can't afford to keep having these types of calls. I was here two weeks for a similar incident. Seems like things keep getting worse."

"So no charges then?"

"Ah, no," he shook his head while looking at the woman standing in front of her van with red French fry cartons still lingering on the ground around her. "I think it's best we have her clean up her mess and get her on her way. I'll talk to her next. As for your son, though, I know you have him work here to keep him out of trouble but sir...this isn't working. So far, he's hasn't hurt anyone but I'm afraid that's only a matter of time." Pointing to the house door, he said, "He's either a very good liar or there's something else going on here. He really doesn't remember yelling at the woman? He also didn't remember kicking the dog the last time I was here."

"Among other things, he has multiple personality disorder. The counselor tells me he doesn't really remember some of the things he's done at all. It's like he wasn't even there. Someone else was. I know it's hard to understand," his father said with a shudder.

Lincoln gave him a moment, fearing the old man might break down. "He seems to like to clean things. Can you have him maybe just take care of the grounds around here instead of interacting with people? Keep him away from the customers. There's a lot of blackberry bushes around back along the highway; can you have him tackle those instead? Anything else to keep him busy other than interacting with the customers."

"Yeah, I can have him do that. Good suggestion."

"I only say that because Mr. Campos, if I have to keep coming out here, I may have to take him away. That and it would be a tragedy if he did hurt someone. Not only for the victim but also for him. You'd likely be separated."

The old man nodded, at a loss for words. He appeared to shake with a sob. "I just don't know what to do with him anymore," he finally said.

It was truly a sad situation for the old man. Patting him on the shoulder was all he could do to console the old man. "Try to keep him busy. If you need our help, please call. I'll go and talk to this lady here and get her on her way."

The old man wiped his nose and went back inside the house after waving goodbye.

On his way back to the gas station, a car pulled in opposite the blue van and an attractive lady wearing dark-framed glasses and a dark bun stepped out. She glanced up at him as he crossed the pavement. Momentarily mesmerized, he finally nodded at her to avoid looking like a stalker. She smiled at him briefly as she slid her glasses up the bridge of her nose and began fueling her car. He cleared his throat and diverted his attention back to the not-so-attractive lady near the van.

"Ma'am, you need to pick up your discarded property, please. I'll wait here until you do, then you can leave."

"Aren't you going to charge him for assault?"

Shaking his head, he replied, "Ma'am, if I do, I'll also have to charge you for littering. This isn't your personal trashcan. You need to clean out your van at your home. The cans here are for convenience and disposal of a little trash, not cleaning out a mess such as this."

"But he assaulted me!"

"No, he didn't from the witness's testimony. He yelled at you for sure. You were unloading what I suspect is a few months' worth of trash here. You need to pick it up and you need to leave."

She stepped closer and squinted her eyes at him while shoving a pudgy index finger at him. "This is why people hate cops."

With a straight face he only said, "Pick it up or I'll issue a citation."

Not the reaction she thought she would get, so she backed away. It took great effort for her to bend over just to pick up the red French fry cartons lingering near her tire. Sneering at him, she went to the next, what looked like a greasy breakfast sandwich wrapper, and had to put her foot on it to keep it from flapping away from her in the warm breeze. She picked most of the trash with great effort as well, and he waited for her to track down three more pieces before he lost his patience and decided to pitch in and give her a hand. If he didn't he'd have to wait for more than half an hour at this rate for her to pick up all the strewn garbage. After tracking down several unused white napkins trying to take flight once again from the hot asphalt, he returned several pieces of trash to find that she'd stopped picking it up and stood by her van waiting for him to do her work for her as sweat drained down the sides of her face.

Lincoln watched and couldn't help noticing the pretty lady's left hand bore no symbol of commitment as she gassed up opposite them. "Dang," he said to himself, wishing he could go over and introduce himself.

"I shouldn't have to do this," the fast food aficionado said.

Lincoln diverted his attention back to the task at hand and shook his head at the litterbug's progress and finally said. "All right, you're free to go. I'd advise you to use one of the many other gas stations nearby. If you continue to come here and cause problems the owner can and will file a trespassing notice and that'll make this a criminal matter. These facilities are for pumping gas, not your personal garbage station."

Her sweaty face turned red with humiliation again. As customers looked at them curiously, she got into her van and drove away. When she left, he was frustrated to see that the pretty lady had also left the scene.

"Just my luck," he muttered.

Remembering what Campos said earlier about worms breeding from trash, he picked up the rest of the refuse littering the ground: crunched white paper straw holders, empty crushed jumbo soda cups, more big hamburger wrappers, corrugated hamburger containers, and burrito wrappers with melted faux cheese still stuck to them. Afterwards, he wished he'd put on his gloves before beginning. His hands slimy with fast food grease, he headed back to his squad car and opened the back where he kept sanitary wipes and cleaned up before getting inside and inputting the information inside the system.

"How you doing, buddy?" he asked Enzo, who was cool and collected then started growling low and ominously out the front window. When Officer Asher looked he saw the younger Campos walking outside with a hatchet in his hand, swinging it back and forth as he headed toward the blackberry bushes behind the service station. Senior Campos stood on the porch of the house and waved to Officer Asher. He waved back and nodded but returned his gaze to Campos, who swung the hatchet with a firm grip then split the air as he walked away. "Hmmm...I wonder if that was such a good idea," he said to Enzo.

# 5

## WONG

Staring at the ceiling, Fan Wong's mind only reflected his sister's anguished face with the knife blade resting against her jaw. She was a quiet girl and the only one who ever made him smile. While he was intelligent, she was creative. Fan loved his sister very much. Saving her as well as his parents was what he would do. There was no real choice in the matter; they would all die soon anyway by his calculations. In this way, Fan was buying time with them. A little more time to say the things he would regret not saying if they'd died by the hands of the terrorists.

Instead, he would be free to return home with them, where he would wait for the weapon he helped to create as it was set free and at least knowing he was with his family, they would meet death together. No one would ever know he was the cause or had anything to do with the exchange. Only his family would be aware of something he had to exchange for them, but they'd never know the real truth.

It rained instead of snowed as Fan walked from his apartment into work. The overcast gray sky hung low, pelting him with water droplets. By the time he made it inside the building, his hair was drenched and his white shirt, now damp, clung to his skin.

"Hello Fan," the receptionist said, though he walked past her without even acknowledging the greeting.

On the third floor, he put his briefcase away and donned his lab coat, covertly slipping an empty glass vial into his coat pocket. He set to work, going through the motions like any other day, though this day instead of being lost in thought, he was sweating bullets. Beads formed on his forehead and his hands. Continuously, he wiped them away and when another lab tech noticed, he said, "Are you okay, Fan?"

"Ah, yes." He tried a brief smile in order to fool the man.

Once again, he worked and at an interval when he would normally put a sample into the refrigeration unit, he slipped the virulent one out, siphoned off a few cc's and injected that into the vial in his pocket. He replaced the unit, sanitized the area and left for his lunch break.

With his eye on the clock, Fan brought his lunch outside to the bench in the park. A man with an umbrella awaited him. When he met him, they sat down on the damp bench. Fan had the vial filled with the deadly fluid in his shirt pocket now. The whole time, he felt the weight of it there. Such a small thing and yet so very deadly.

"My family?" Fan said shortly after.

The man on the bench next to him handed him an iPad displaying a video. He pressed play and watched as a van pulled up in front of his home. His family stepped out. His mother held his sister close to her side, clenching her daughter. His father looked confused as he ushered his wife and child into the staircase leading up to their apartment building, eager to separate his family from these men. The video stayed on them as they walked the staircase, opened their apartment door and closed it behind them.

Fan's heart rate settled a little. Reaching into his shirt pocket, he pulled out the vial and held the tip with two fingers as the liquid precariously suspended below.

Suddenly, the man with the iPad looked frightened and even moved away. "You don't have a better container?"

"No, it would draw too much suspicion."

The extortionist reached for the vial with his palm up. Fan laid the harbinger of death down in the center of his spread hand.

"I wouldn't open that if I were you."

The man realized it was a serious warning and all threats aside, he agreed. The terror in his brown eyes was plain to see.

"It's what you wanted?" Fan asked rhetorically.

"Yes."

Fan stood. "You will leave my family and me alone now?"

The man didn't answer. Instead he'd cupped another hand over the first, beads of sweat forming on his forehead despite the cold temperature; he stood and walked away.

Fan stared after his tormentor for a bit without having his answer. Leaving the park, Fan didn't return to work. Instead, he went back to his apartment and grabbed his bicycle, heading to his family home. Whatever happened with the man and the vial was no longer his concern. He'd paid the price to see his family for a little longer and that was all he cared about now. Pedaling away, he soon joined a crowd of bicycle commuters, undistinguishable from the rest, all busily about their day.

# 6

## CLARISSE

**R**arely did she receive a text message or call on the spare phone, although she was never without it; the dead weight went wherever she did, alongside the one that buzzed regularly with texts from colleges and calls from acquaintances. Clarisse never kept friends. She was a loner for the most part, never wanting the reciprocal response present in a friendship, the responsibility too daunting to her. The fact that she lived and breathed her work was also a deterrent from having close friends. But mostly, it was the prediction of things to come that lessened her interest in anyone who she might have to lose in time to come.

The message had read "Code Two" and that meant for her and a select few to meet, now. Meeting *where* wasn't readily explained. She texted back an inquiry code as expected, along with her personal password identifying her as the recipient. Again, the phone vibrated and when she picked it up, an address and time were listed in the field of encrypted characters. The message automatically deleted ten seconds after she read it and committed it to memory as she drove in to work. She had until later this evening before she would meet at the given address. Her contact was a man named Dalton and his partner was Rick. She mostly conferred with Rick as the communications and technology officer but Dalton was the lead of this side project that she put a lot of time and effort into.

It wasn't that she was scared of the news or a conspiracy theorist at heart. Clarisse knew things. Things only someone who works for the government could fear. She'd been approached recently through a Russian conduit, she suspected feeling her out for information. Being a scientist in virology wasn't a benefit in these times; it was a curse and one that she was smart enough to realize made her a target for the worst of crimes against humanity. She suspected that around the globe, anyone with her knowledge and skills was being hounded by the secret society of nations to do harm. A harm that would undo society as they knew it. To protect herself, she limited her liabilities. She had no friends or family for them to use against her as it was. Her elderly parents had died a decade before, having had her as their only child. It was a fate she often felt a loss for, but now she saw the silver lining of such an existence. Had she had a sibling or lover, they could easily use that person to get to her.

In her spare time, she began to prepare, knowing it was only a matter of time. Call her crazy but being in her position, where a virologist could be used to develop a weapon of mass destruction, proved to her how vulnerable society was and how fleeting hope had become in the political climate meant to catch fire with the next shooting, terrorist attack, or election.

The group she had carefully researched before entering the year before met randomly and planned in secret. They agreed on a few major principles, including absolute secrecy and a low number of members. Everyone who joined brought a unique set of skills. They'd met a few times already, made plans and established the order of things and a location that they were developing, but only a few people knew of the exact location. For her part, she set up a storage unit and had slowly filled it with the items she would need as their chief medical officer and scientist. Without establishing any detectable routine, she filled an SUV stored in the facility with all the items she would need. Recently receiving a few more essentials delivered to her unmarked UPS store address under an assumed name, she had added a few more items to the stock in the SUV. These items were new technology meant to keep electronics going in case of a lack of battery power or an EMP. For larger equipment, she gave the model number and list of items she would need, like a mobile containment unit, to Rick to acquire. She had no idea how he was able to get the isolation unit undetected, and she didn't ask, but the last time she'd checked he had acquired everything on her list. She was impressed and had more confidence in the process after he'd proved to her that they meant what they said. "*Anything* you need," Dalton had told her. "And we'll do our best to obtain."

She'd said, "If you're serious about this...here's my list." Apparently, they were serious. Now her concern was the Code 2. That meant there was reasonable suspicion in the intel community that a risk was detected. If anyone called a Code 5, that was imminent and they needed to head to their location without contacting anyone else. That meant the end. Leave it all behind. This was it without a doubt. *This* is not a drill.

Only a few were in the position to call a Code 5. She was one. The others were either in intel or military and had access to the knowledge needed to warn when the end was near.

It might only take a second to warn the others and in her heart of hearts, it wasn't fool proof. To her, if they made it to that stage of things, it probably was already too late. Everyone would die trying to make it into their safe zone.

She hoped not but over two months had gone by since she'd even heard a rattle from the phone, until this morning, and that was a scary sign.

At work, she went about her day as normal. Donning her lab coat, she kept both phones inside the front pockets with her at all times, and the weight swung against her thigh as she walked, reminding her of the danger. Busily working, with her eyes staring through a microscope, she didn't notice her boss standing next to her. He touched her arm. "Dr. Smarting, we have a meeting in five minutes. Can you attend?"

"Uh...I'm a little busy here," she said, not wanting to waste her time sitting through a boring meeting when she had work to do, but the look on his face said he had concerns and they weren't trivial. She swallowed. "But I can take a break. Sure. Staff room?" she asked him.

"No. My office," he said and walked out of the lab, his shoulders hunched with a look as if the burdens of the world weighed him down.

*Something's up*, she thought and went back to work. After writing down a few findings and tossing her contaminated slides into the secure sanitizer, she took off her gloves and tossed them into the trash on her way out of the lab after sanitizing.

The door to her boss's office was closed. When he swung the door open, another man was seated in one of the chrome chairs before the desk. He was an elderly man, in his near eighties, she suspected. She knew him as Mr. Claiborne.

He smiled up at her as she took the seat next him.

As she was the chief virologist, she wondered why more weren't invited. *This must be something big or they'd have called a staff meeting.*

"Hi Dr. Smarting. Glad you could join us," Mr. Claiborne, her boss's superior, said, his voice almost a whisper. He suffered from emphysema but was still brilliant and worth his time in the lab.

"I'll not keep you for long. This is a private meeting," her boss said. "It's a briefing, really." They sat down. He looked to the other man seated next to her with concern. "There's been a development. It seems the Chinese have succeeded in obtaining a new bioweapon."

She wasn't surprised; they'd done it before. *Heck, we have them as well,* she thought, even though the prospect was frightening. There was a silence then, to let that news sink in. "So do we; we all know that. Did they develop it? Or was it a pay to play kind of thing? What are their intentions, do you think?"

"That, we don't yet know."

"How do you know this is a new one?" Clarisse asked.

"We don't for certain. We got a call from Washington. They're positive they have a new, advanced avian flu. No one knows for sure."

*How can that be?* Clarisse thought. "They're just saying they have a bioweapon? And bragging about it? That's not like the Chinese. That's more like the North Koreans."

Her boss nodded.

She looked to the two men, one then the other. All eyes were on her. *What are these guys getting at?* "Well, it wasn't me. If you suspect I helped develop it, you're dead wrong."

"Oh, we know it wasn't *you*," her boss said. "We're just letting you know that we have to implement security features required by the government."

"Oh, that's a given. What kind of bioweapon do you think they have and who specifically do you think developed it? There's only a few of us truly capable," Clarisse said and hoped her assumptions were true. More than a few in-the-know was a truly frightening concept.

"All questions we have no answers for. If intel knows, they're not telling us," her boss said, leaning back in his chair with his hands held wide to the unknown.

She nodded. "So we don't know what it is, therefore we have no idea what kind of vaccine we'll need if they use it."

"Exactly," her boss said and leaned back in his chair with his hands behind his head this time. It was a posture of a relaxed man. In a way his gesture told her, *There's nothing we can do about this so why try?*

Confused, she said, "Are they trying to intercept it? Have they demanded something in exchange?"

"No. Intel sent a video to Washington showing a tiny vial exchanged somewhere in China and it's now in their possession; nothing more."

"Whose possession?" she asked.

The man next to her, who'd remained silent, spoke up. "We're not sure."

She shook her head and leaned against her seat. Now she understood the defeatist posture but then again, she couldn't do that for long. She wasn't one to lie down and take whatever came her way submissively.

After a pause, Clarisse spoke her thoughts out loud. "They know this puts them at risk. Well, I say we examine the video to see if we can determine the contents of the vial. Will they let us look at it?"

"No, I've already asked," her boss said.

Letting out a frustrated breath, Clarisse said, "Can they describe the liquid? I'm assuming it's a liquid."

"They said it's a clear liquid, no distinguishable color or texture. Though the film was from quite a distance."

"Could be anything then," Clarisse speculated.

"Yeah, and it could be water for all we know."

"You think it's possibly a hoax?" Clarisse said.

"Why? I have no idea, but I have no control over the situation." He spread his hands out wide. "They asked for you, you know?"

She pushed her glasses up the bridge of her nose and shook her head. "I don't want to live in D. C. or anywhere around a government agency. I'm happy where I am."

Her boss nodded. "I thought so, but I had to mention it. They wanted to you to fly out today. I told them you were working on something and asked what good it would do to have you go there to look at a video just to come to the same futile conclusions."

"Thanks," she said. "I've worked for them for most of my life. I prefer to stay here."

He nodded again. "I thought so."

"Anything else?" she asked, not understanding why they even called this meeting.

"No. There's nothing we can do about it, if they do in fact have a bioweapon. That's it."

Curiously, the man next to her said no more during the whole exchange. She glanced at him again, as if giving him the chance to engage in the conversation, and then back at her boss. She wasn't sure where the defeatist attitude was coming from. Circular logic wasn't in her own portfolio. "There's always something we can do. Fight, for instance. Don't take it lying down."

"Well, Clarisse, when you get to be my age, you look at the world a little differently."

That was it. She knew there was no changing the man's attitude.

"All right, well, I've got a few more things to do before the end of the day. Please keep me informed of any new developments."

The gentleman next to her smiled and nodded his head as she rose from her chair.

"I certainly will. Thank you, Dr. Smarting," her boss said.

She smiled but shook her head on her way back to her lab with a heavy heart. This warning was something she could call her own Code 2 in to the group for but since she was meeting with them anyway she refrained from doing so. For all she knew, they were already informed and that was the very reason they were meeting later this evening. As she sat down again at her lab table, she conceded in her own mind that this was in fact probably the reason. Both her contacts, Dalton and Rick, seemed to know things before even she was aware. She didn't know how that was true with her own contacts, and she didn't want to know.

After work, instead of heading home she started the long drive to the next town north and pulled into the storage unit where she kept her *ready to go* equipment. While inside the dark storage unit, she thought of the day's events so far and had the feeling that she might be using the equipment sooner rather than later. After putting the new items inside, she then headed off to the address given to her. An hour later, she pulled up to a little prefab building in a little town near Carnation, Washington. Out in a farmer's field, there was only the little white prefab building and a few other vehicles that were parked out front. Always their meetings were like this, in secret, in a new location, at differing hours and different days. Never the same spot or same time. She knocked on the door and Rick opened it.

"Hello Doc. Glad, you could join us," he said.

"Please, call me Clarisse. We agreed to go by first names last time."

He nodded and ushered her inside closing the door behind her.

"Hello," Dalton said.

"Hi," she said and sat at a desk filled with schematic papers, turning the swivel chair to face them. She assumed the work area was possibly a contractor's or farmer's; she had no idea.

"Let's get right to the point," Dalton said. "I've received intel from my sources that there's a major bioweapon in the hands of the Chinese and apparently it's up for sale. No one knows yet where or how they obtained the weapon but the intel suggests it's the real deal. We may have to move our plans up a little if this is true. But I also want to address this specific threat and how we're going to deal with it."

Clarisse let out a frustrated breath.

"Is there something you know?" Dalton asked.

"Uh, I can't. I've got a security clearance, as you know, but I will tell you this: I don't have any *additional* information."

They all regarded her. "That's a confirmation of what I just told you."

She smiled.

"I won't ask," Dalton said. "So that leaves us with an imminent bio terror threat. Let's step it up. Hypothetically, what do we need to do to mitigate the effects of this particular threat?"

"Um, we need the quarantine building up and ready to go. As we call people in, they will have to go through the chamber before being let into the camp itself. There's no way around that."

"But that could leave some of our members stranded while they're waiting their turn to get through," Rick said.

"Can you get more than one quarantine unit?" she asked Rick.

"I'll try," he said.

"I also need the lab set up. The only way around this is to obtain a sample and begin developing a vaccine if possible."

"Okay, we'll get started. We already have several caches in place in various locations in case something happens to the first site."

She liked the way Dalton thought. The man had contingencies for his contingencies in mind.

"I would really also like to ensure we have a few more medical staff included. I hope I'm not the only one. If this turns out to be a bio threat situation, I'll need help."

Rick piped up, "One of our participants is an EMS officer. I've served with him most of my career. He's a good buddy of mine."

"That's helpful; would be nice if we had more."

Dalton shook his head. "We're at capacity for members now. We've vetted everyone thoroughly. I don't want to invite any more this late in the game and risk exposure."

It was a grave statement to make, a simple one but grave.

"That makes us around what, a hundred?" Rick asked.

"Yeah," Dalton said and they all sat in thought for a time.

"There's only so much we can do, guys. Much larger and we risk exposing ourselves," Rick said.

"I would expect losing 20% in this particular scenario. People will inevitably risk exposure on their way in, one way or another," she said.

"Let's hope it's not that virulent," Dalton said and looked at his watch.

"If it's weaponized, it's virulent," she said.

Dalton looked up from his watch, "Okay, last one in is first one out. Bye Clarisse."

With her lips in a straight line, Clarisse gave them both a poignant stare. "This time, it's real. I have a really bad feeling about this one." With that she left, loving that they kept the meeting to fifteen minutes. She left them with the knowledge that the risk of a bioweapon was for real, not only confirmed by her own employer, but also the secret group she was a member of.

On the drive home, she went through all her preparations mentally and hoped she'd thought of every contingency if this were the catalyst put into place like she suspected. Such a heavy burden to bear. She had only one chance to get it right if this threat was the catalyst to light the blaze she sensed was coming like the blaze of a forest fire through dry tinder.

## 7

# LINCOLN

By the end of the day, Officer Asher and Enzo pulled into the station. Despite the high temperatures it had been a relatively slow day. Perhaps the heat was now making everyone calm and they'd finally learned that in order to cool off in the hottest part of the day, one only needed to stay still, like a siesta. They were at the end of September now...certainly cooler days were ahead of them.

As he came through the door, he was curious about what'd happened to the thief he'd chased down the other day and brought to the hospital. As Lincoln approached the day clerk, Ms. Campbell, he wondered if she'd just pulled an all-nighter. Her hair was usually up in a blonde swirl and pinned at the back of her head like something out of Laverne and Shirley, but this time it was undone, with strands flying all over in the wind coming from the nearby desk fans. Being in her fifties now, she mostly manned the desks and was well respected by all the officers. She'd easily let you know what was what with a voice as gravely as a big man's if you stepped out of line.

"Hey Ms. Campbell, can you tell me what happened to the guy we brought into Harborview? Has anyone picked him up yet?"

After covering her mouth and hacking out a cough before she

spoke and whipping away the phlegm, the dispatcher looked at him with confusion, or rather, he always had the impression she thought he was an imbecile. "Darlin', you didn't hear?"

"Hear what?"

She cleared her throat of a wracking cough again before she spoke. "Death in custody. They called and said the fever was that virus that's been going around. They're running tests. Seems it's pretty bad."

"He's dead? But it was just a fever when I brought him in. Did it have anything to do with the bite?" he said, feeling stuck on the first part of the conversation.

She picked up a folder and spun on her seat. "He probably had a compromised immune system or some other underlying cause. I hope you didn't pick it up, whatever it was. It's going around along with this heat and it's making us all miserable. When everyone gets back to work, things will get back to normal, which means you and Officer Enzo will be under investigation."

He watched her put the folder in a file cabinet, her movements slow, agonizing. "Don't take this wrong, Ms. Campbell, but you don't look so good yourself. Maybe you should go home and rest."

"I can't; the other two dispatchers have called in sick already. They beat me to it."

"I expect there will be a few investigations going on once every-thing gets back to normal. Are they as sick as you? Is it the same thing?"

She shook her head in defeat. "I don't know. I just know that if I can walk, I can work. That's why I'm here."

"I understand but if it's contagious, you ought to stay home, Ms. Campbell."

She gave him a flustered look, somewhat offended. "And who else are you going to call in to take over?"

Staring at her blankly, he hadn't a clue.

And she knew it. "I'll be fine. Nothing I can't handle," she said through her husky voice.

He and Enzo were soon off duty and headed home. It seemed as if the day were nothing more than a blur of heat-induced arguments. When he pulled up into the driveway of the one-level house rambler with a backyard big enough for Enzo to run around in, which was as much as he could afford on his salary with the high residential prices in Seattle, he saw his sister's white Camry sitting in the inclined driveway. She'd parked at an angle again, making it impossible for him to pull his squad car in normally, so he had to park alongside the road, in front of the house, instead.

"Man, that girl," he said to Enzo when he put the car in park. "Come on Enzo, I hope she started dinner at least."

The second he walked into the foyer, which was only called so because there was a landing of tiles in a grid as soon as you walked through the doorway, he smelled a lack of anything cooking in the kitchen. "Hell to the no," he remarked to Enzo.

"Linc," Paige called from her bedroom.

"Yeah, what's up?" he said as he removed his gear, placing his weapon in a bio safe in the hall closet, along with the rest of his gear.

"I have to go out. I have a date."

"Hey, I thought we agreed no dating until you were through with the summer quarter. Is this the same guy you were with the other night?"

"You agreed. I did not agree," she said, rolling her eyes at him.

He shook his head. "Is he picking you up?" he yelled over the intermittent sound of a blow-dryer. Suddenly he choked on girl's perfume permeating the thick, moist shower air, something he loathed, especially on his little sister. "Can you spray that stuff outside, please? Smells like a bordello in here," he said as he walked over and leaned against her bathroom doorjamb. She was dressed in a skimpy little white eyelet sundress with spaghetti straps. He knew he shouldn't but he couldn't help himself. "Paige, can you please wear a sweater over that?"

Paige snarled at him. "Are you kidding? It's like 120 degrees out there. Get outta my space. What do you want?"

Taking a breath through his mouth to avoid inhaling the perfume, he said, "I asked...is he picking you up?"

Cutting her eyes away, she said, "No, I don't want you to scare him off."

"Paige, don't date someone you're afraid to bring home to meet me. That's a warning he's not worth your time."

"Don't tell me what to *do*," she said and slammed the bathroom door.

"*Ugh! Sisters!*" Pressing his lips together in a straight line, he stomped to the back door and let Enzo out and waited for him to come back, not wanting to leave him outside in the broiling weather any longer than it took to do his business. Once they were inside again, Linc watched as Enzo found the air conditioner vent on the living room floor and curled up nearby. "You got the right idea, buddy," Lincoln said as he went into his room and changed into shorts and a light t-shirt. That's when he heard the sound of Paige slipping out the front door. "Paige!" he yelled, but it was too late. She was already backing down the driveway with her head looking over her shoulder as he opened the front door and watched her go.

She never acknowledged he was even there standing in the front of the house, even though he suspected she knew he was there. "Sheesh," he said and grabbed his keys, braving the hot cement with his bare feet, and pulled his car into his usual parking spot while he was out there, tempted to park at an angle as well. *That girl needs a taste of her own treatment.*

Back inside, he popped a Hearty Man TV Dinner into the microwave. The label promised fried chicken *just like mom's*, mashed potatoes and green beans. "They lie," he said to Enzo, who carefully watched him in the kitchen. "Never like mom used to make." When he heard the ding of the microwave he filled Enzo's food and water bowl and then took his own dinner into the living room, along with a cold beer, propped his bare feet up on the coffee table and used the remote to turn on the television while he propped the hot TV dinner on his lap with plenty of napkins. He flipped on the news channel and listened to the talking heads, not really taking in what they were saying, while he tried to use his fork on the chicken. The crispy thigh was like a dry inferno, so instead of using his fingers, he used the fork and plopped the piece into his mouth and then immediately regretted that the moment he did, nearly searing his tongue off. He took a quick swig of his beer, feeling the foam expand in his mouth, and then decided to let his meal cool a bit before attempting another bite, while he turned up the volume on the television.

"The World Health Organization has issued a level nine on the Influenza Risk Assessment Tool (IRAT), which classifies this flu incident as 'high risk' and warns that this is a highly virulent bird flu that has already taken the lives of eleven people around the world. Not exactly an epidemic: five cases in China, though there may be more, as they have a tendency to vastly underreport; three confirmed cases in Europe and three here in the United States so far.

"Dr. Elijah Becker, please tell us what we're actually dealing with."

"A level nine certainly sounds grave but really, we have nothing to fear. Schools will shut down for a few days to help contain the spread. Those affected will be quarantined. This isn't unlike the Ebola scare from a few years ago. All the precautions were unfounded in the end. Though there was panic at first, we actually had it under control, so what the media can do this time is to keep calm and put out a confident message."

"This isn't exactly like the Ebola virus though. This one *is* airborne, correct?"

The doctor put up his hands in a display of caution. "While this particular virus is technically airborne," he said in air-quotes, "there's no reason why we can't handle it effectively.'" He laughed. "Give our medical community some credit. Come on, this isn't 1918. We've made huge advances in healthcare since that time. We've contained those who are affected and we have units ready to deploy at a moment's notice. This isn't going to be a pandemic."

Those last seven words replayed in Linc's mind like an echo repeating on the hot, muggy wind. It wasn't that he doubted the expert's words. He believed the expert believed what he was saying; he just didn't have the same conviction. Then Linc flashed on touching the thief's forehead and feeling the heat emanating from the man's skull. He'd practically carried him into the hospital and breathed in the same air he did. If the thief had the same virus…he knew he'd already been exposed, if not from the thief then from the dispatcher at the precinct today or the myriad of people he came in close personal contact with daily. If this bird flu was that contagious… hell, he already had it and because he already felt grimy and greasy from the fried chicken on his fingers, he couldn't help but go to the kitchen and toss what was left into the trash and wash his hands a little extra under the hot spray of the faucet. Rarely did he grab a second beer from the fridge in the evening but on his way out of the kitchen he convinced himself that it didn't matter and hell, it was hot.

He and his partner watched a little more television that night, not really into the program about society turning into zombies, when he checked the time on his phone. Paige still wasn't home. "Damn, girl, it's past midnight." Though he couldn't really give her a hard time about it anymore. He reached for the remote and shut off the television, turned on the outside lights, set the alarm and went to bed. Enzo curled up on his bed on the floor beside him and before long it was Linc who waited to hear his partner's snores before he drifted off to sleep himself.

# 8

# CLARISSE

A few days later, Clarisse refilled her cat's water bowl and added fresh food to the other side until the kibble over-flowed to the floor, knowing she'd probably work late into the night. He ate hungrily, chewing each kernel with the side of his jaw, methodically, as she ran her hand along the back of his fur, his tail taut in her hand at the tip. "Miss me?" she asked him and when he didn't break stride chewing away she said, "I didn't think so."

Shortly afterward, she found herself sitting on her stool at the lab table again. The Seattle drive had become so monotonous she barely remembered it anymore except for her brief stop for gas. Nothing more was mentioned about the alarming intel from days before. Only a few murmurings in the news of bird flu and quarantine procedures for livestock. Then suddenly someone in a lab coat swung open the door so hard, it bounced off the outer wall. "Clarisse, have you heard?" The voice belonged to a young man she knew as Cameron who wore thin silver-rimmed glasses. He was always the one to inform the others of work gossip camouflaged as pertinent information.

"Heard what?"

"Can't you hear the news in here?"

The television volume blared in from the corridor leading to her lab. She was annoyed; the staff knew she liked a quiet working environment where she encouraged headphones and iPhones, and the talking heads weren't something she'd allowed in her lab on a regular basis. They were aware of this policy so whatever it was, it had to be important enough to disregard her wrath.

After cleaning up, she went out into the corridor, where she found practically the entire office huddled around the overhead television in the breakroom. She expected to find the latest terror attack or attempted assassination blazing the television waves. Frightened looks from her colleagues brought her to read the headlines streaming across the bottom of the screen. "Unconfirmed reports of a Weaponized Bird Flu Pandemic coming in from China."

"Is it true?" asked the front desk receptionist. Her question was directed at Clarisse. Several heads turned in her direction.

She raised her shoulders in a silent noncommittal gesture, and the heads turned quickly back to the television once they realized there were no answers coming from Clarisse. She stood at the back of the crowd and exited the break room. She reached her hand into her pocket and on her way out the door to the parking lot and her car, she texted the words "Code 5" and then found her thumb hovering over the send button. She stopped then, in between this pivotal moment. Looking toward her Camry, she then looked back at the building's entrance doors. Was this really it? What if she was wrong? Then, diverting her attention to the horizon...What if she was right? She sent the message.

There was no going home now. She walked quickly to her car. "I'm so sorry," she said, the thought of her cat dying of starvation in her locked apartment where she'd left him that morning bringing tears to her eyes. As she drove north through Seattle in the drizzling rain and with a nearly full tank of gas, she never stopped, not even once.

# 9

# LINCOLN

H is morning coffee wasn't doing it for him today. Dragging his ass was an understatement. "Come on, Enzo," he whispered as he picked up his equipment for the day, and his travel mug. "Let's get going," he said in the same low tone with an armload, quietly walking out the door.

When he stepped outside the first thing that hit him was the warm, humid breeze and cloudy gray sky, then he expected to see Paige's car parked out front, possibly blocking his way as usual. He'd have to drag her out of bed to make her move it again, like he'd done so many times before. Except when he looked, he didn't see her car at all. This was after he'd tried to keep the noise down like he did every morning getting ready, out of respect for the sleeping, or passed out, except his sister wasn't exactly sleeping...not in his house, anyway.

"Dammit, Paige," he said as he let Enzo into the back seat. He shut the door and then pulled out his phone. "No texts. So much trouble," he mumbled and just as he was about to call her, his phone rang, but looking at the screen, it wasn't her calling him after all. It was actually the pager on his waistband buzzing. He looked at the tiny screen... Alpha Bravo Schedule – days. "Dammit." Then his phone buzzed in his hand.

"Hello?" he answered not too graciously as he opened his own door and sat inside, all the while thinking of how he would strangle his little sister the next time he saw her. *Can't I just lock her in her room? Why would that be illegal?*

"Hey Lincoln, we've got some problems, and we're short-staffed..."

"Yeah, I just got the text."

Instead of pulling into the precinct parking lot, Lincoln went straight to Harborview Medical Center, though he had a hard time finding a place to park. There were cars double-parked everywhere and crowds of people in the way of the turnaround drop-off area. "This is not good," he said to Enzo as he stared out the window at the increasing crowd with car horns blaring in the distance.

Stepping out of his vehicle, he took Enzo with him by the leash and said, "What's going on here?" in an even tone to the first person who looked halfway alert—a man standing nearby in the moist heat of the morning wearing a light blue t-shirt and white plaid board shorts in Birkenstock sandals. Except that the person was in the midst of a coughing fit. When the man looked up at him, his eyes were draining down his face. He couldn't seem to catch his breath. He finally put his hands on his hips in an attempt to fake his wellness, jutting his chin toward the hospital lobby.

"Ah," he said and pointed at the emergency room, "they closed their doors. They're not taking any more patients and what's worse," he cleared his throat again, "my wife's in there. I checked her in last night and went back to check on my kids. They're also sick with this stuff and when I got back here, they won't let anyone in or out. She's not answering her phone either. I don't know what's going on. Is this some kind of quarantine?"

"I don't know, sir," Lincoln said and the concerned husband was hit again with a wave of wracking coughs. His coughing alerted Enzo a bit and when he jerked, Lincoln said, "Do me a favor, sir, please go take a seat in your car. You're not well, either. Hey, don't fall over," he said as the man began to sway. He had to catch him by the forearm as he started falling to the ground.

"Whoa, sorry, I'm a little lightheaded. I think...I'm okay now," he said. "Thanks, I'll go sit in my car now."

"You won't do your family any good if you're also wearing yourself out," Lincoln said as he watched the man make his way back to the parking lot, bearing his weight on other vehicles as he went. He didn't see which vehicle he got into though, because suddenly there was an air horn blown near the front doors of the emergency room sliders.

"Please move away from the entrance. The hospital has closed. If you have family members inside we will give you information soon. No one is allowed in or out of this facility now. We are under a mandatory quarantine. Again, please move away from the entrance doors."

But they weren't moving away. And a few of the members of the crowd began to shout. One father carrying a child in his arms rushed to the nurse with the bullhorn but before he got there the nurse stepped inside the glass doors and locked the doors shut.

"What in the hell?" Lincoln said and began walking toward the entrance himself.

"She's dying. Let me in!" the man yelled at the nurse through the glass.

Though muffled through the doorway, the nurse in dark berry scrubs was near tears as she replied, "I'm sorry. We're under quarantine. We can't take her."

"She's going to die. She can't breathe!" he begged.

Lincoln and Enzo watched the man's back as he yelled the words, sobs catching in between them.

"Excuse me," Lincoln said as he walked through the crowd. Despite their situation, most of the people were reluctant to move until they saw the uniform, and the police dog helped too.

When he finally made it up the doorway, the man still stood there, holding his unconscious child in his arms.

"What's going on here?" Lincoln said cautiously.

The man turned. And it wasn't the situation that first shocked him. It was a glimpse of the girl with the long blonde hair that caught his attention before he had a chance to say anything. Her bloodshot brown eyes were open and had a dull, glassy cast. She was about nine or ten, he guessed. Her father must have been struggling to carry her weight around but he didn't look down at her. He seemed to avoid the act at all costs, and Lincoln knew why. Dried blood trickled from the corner of her mouth and out of her nose. She'd been dead for about an hour or so.

Lincoln looked directly at the nurse through the glass door then. She was visibly shaking with sobs. She looked back at him and shook her head, her chest heaving, and she too started coughing. As Lincoln's view went past her, he saw patients lining the hallways on cots inside, in wheelchairs and in the waiting room. There were many more leaning over in chairs, wracked with coughs; many were on the floor lining the walls. She was right...they couldn't take any more patients. They were overrun.

Reaching for his mic on his shoulder, Lincoln called into the station. "Need backup at Harborview Med." He waited for a response and when none came right away, he tried again.

Finally, the dispatcher's voice came over at a high clip. "No units available. Ordered to seal off county border. All health facilities overrun."

What the heck? How the hell did this happen so fast?

As Lincoln stepped away from the crowd, the man still stood staring through the glass, holding his dead daughter in his arms.

That's when Lincoln coughed and caught himself. He looked down at the phlegm in his hand and then at Enzo looking back up at him, his eyes affixed to his.

"Come on, buddy. Let's go."

There was no use ordering these people home; they were there for the duration, he suspected. Or the end...he wasn't sure. A helpless wave passed over him as he watched the father again staring down the helpless nurse inside. Tell the man to leave? Where would he go? There was no point in any of this. The only thing he could do now was go to the border as he was ordered and hope to stem the tide coming in.

## 10

### PAIGE

"Linc, finally. Where have you been?" Paige said, her voice frantic.

"Paige, calm down. What's wrong? Where are you?"

"I'm with Trevor. I've been with him all night. He can't breathe... and we were refused at the hospital and there's no one at the Urgent Care. I don't know what to do, Linc. No one will help us. He's turning purple. He can't breathe."

"Paige...don't touch him. Get away from him now. Go home, right now, Paige. I mean it. There's a pan..." he was saying. But she didn't hear the rest. She knew he wasn't going to help them. She simply ended the call.

"Oh my God," she cried. Trevor wheezed next to her in the passenger seat. He'd lost consciousness over an hour ago. "Okay, okay," she said, pushing her blond hair out of her eyes and wiping her tears away. A wave of people passed in front of her car; one of them, a man in a red tee shirt, braced himself, one hand on the hood of her car, one step, another bracing hand, dragging himself along as he looked at her beyond the glass. "What else can I do?" she said out loud to herself.

Thinking of nothing, she decided in the end to do exactly what her brother said, except she was bringing Trevor home too, thinking there had to be something in the medicine chest he kept there. Her biggest fear was losing yet another person she'd come to love.

As soon as the people passed in front of her, she drove on her way home, checking beside her to see if Trevor's chest rose and fell with the next breath. "Please keep breathing."

Then at the next light, she looked over again, waiting to see the rise and fall of his chest. "Trevor?" she yelled. "Trevor?" she screamed again and reached over, grabbing hold of his button-up shirt covered in phlegm and shaking him back and forth. "Trevor, breathe!!!" When nothing happened, she climbed over onto the passenger side, placed her mouth over his and blew breath into him. Over and over, she stopped and waited to see if this worked.

When she finally stopped, the light had turned green. A truck behind her laid on his horn. And there was no breath, no heartbeat, despite her best efforts. The only sound she heard was her own broken heart.

# 11

## LINCOLN

"Paige?" he said when she didn't answer and looked into the phone, seeing that he still had a signal; she'd just hung up on him. He was about to call her back but he was on his way to the roadblock they were establishing on Highway 90 at the edge of the county when his radio sounded. In the distance, he saw a few flashing red lights.

"6113?"

"Yeah," he replied, noting how radio communication protocol had waned in the past few hours.

"We have an urgent call of a home invasion near your location. A female dialed in saying her apartment had been broken into and her husband killed, then the line went dead. Linc, I don't have backup. Is there a way you can divert over to that location?"

"I wish I could. Look, traffic is choked up here. With my lights on, I can barely get through. They don't give a damn. Looks like just as many people are fleeing the county as are coming in. I'm sorry, I can't even get over to the exit ramp, and certainly not in a hurry."

"That's a negative?"

Looking around with his lights and sirens on, traffic blaring horn after horn, he replied, "That's a negative."

"Okay," said the dispatch.

He hung up then, intending to call Paige back, when Enzo barked suddenly, growling at a passing car. Suddenly a car sideswiped him in a slow execution to run Asher into the next lane. Apparently, they'd resorted to bumper cars now. "Seriously?" Asher said. *These people,* he thought, *they have no regard for even the police.* "They're beyond afraid," he said out loud. Looking back at Enzo, he could see the hair on the back of his scruff and end stood straight up. "It's okay, buddy," he said and Enzo looked back at him as if he were nuts. This was definitely not okay. Everyone had lost their minds.

"Paige," he yelled into the phone while maneuvering into the next lane by force. *More than one can play this bumper car thing,* he thought and as he pushed one car way over into the next lane he glared at the driver angrily while he dialed Paige's number again. "Paige, answer, dammit."

He said the words but didn't hear them with the traffic noise so loud. A continuous cacophony of horns blared.

Seattle was forever trying to improve their traffic dilemmas, from stop and go light on-ramps, to toll roads, to massive efforts to force commuters into public transportation. Even so, Seattle remained a gridlocked city. There was no getting around it. Weekends were often spent just simply recovering from road rage and congestion. No one wants to spend their life bumper to bumper, no matter how content you are with the daily rain.

"Hey, get back!" Asher yelled out of his lowered window to a truck trying to edge him away from the roadblock in force, while Enzo barked ferociously. *Screw this,* Asher thought and turned on the PA system and grabbed his mic. "I said, get back." His voice boomed over the traffic noise and seemed to stop several aggressive drivers in their tracks as they inched for any empty space before them.

The driver, a male in his fifties, if Asher had to guess, lowered his eyes immediately and let him through. "These guys have all lost their minds in such a short time," Asher said to Enzo, who appeared to agree with him as he hung his tongue out, keeping an eye on the drivers passing by far too close to their vehicle.

Then he coughed and a sudden surge of congestion hit him, taking him over. With his foot held steady on the brake, his eyes flooded with tears. His phone fell from his hands. Then he wiped his brow, realizing he was burning up, and from more than just the hot, humid temperature. "Damn," he eked out, holding his chest before another wracking wave of coughs hit him. Finally he rolled up the window again and blasted the air conditioner on high. Just two more layers of cars to go and he'd make it to the roadblock. Then Lincoln suddenly ducked at the sound of gunshots ahead.

# 12

## CLARISSE

Shaking his head, Rick said, "I'm sorry, Clarisse. I couldn't get the second unit in time. I've even tried to locate the delivery truck trapped on a highway, but it's too risky to take a crew to retrieve it. Dalton and I just had that discussion."

"I know," Clarisse said as she looked out at the crowd of camping vehicles and people forming in their secluded camp area just outside of the tiny town of Cascade, Washington, waiting to enter the quarantined zone.

"Best laid plans and all. We have to go with first come, first serve before we end up with any fighting. You've got to convey that to them; we're going as fast as we can."

"I will but you know as well as I do, there will be fighting."

"Yes, and make sure they understand that everyone must—and I mean must—stay clear of one another; if they can stay in their vehicles apart from everyone else, that's the best thing. At least a hundred feet. One family at a time...this will take a while."

"I've not seen anyone with symptoms so far."

She snapped at him then, "That doesn't matter, Rick." She pointed out into the group of campers. "At least one of them is exposed; more will contract it right here. We'll be lucky if we can get half of them through without the rest coming down with it. You do have a plan for those exposed?"

Seeing a wave of grief flash over his face, he nodded.

She did too, though silently. "I'm sorry."

"Me too. But they agreed to all the final details and consequences, in writing."

"Are we missing anyone? Everyone's checked in; who's coming in?"

"Yeah, there's a few I'm afraid we've already lost. I just got the last ping by Sam from Montana. He has a young daughter. Apparently, he just lost his wife to breast cancer a few weeks ago, poor guy. And now this. They haven't even had a chance to grieve."

"God, that's awful. How far out are they?"

"He's coming in from Kalispell. With traffic, it might be a few days. He left last night. Has extra fuel on board. He won't stop anywhere along the way."

"Do you have alternate routes for him to take just in case he gets hung up?"

"I do. I'm tracking him."

"Good, I hope they make it in."

"Me too...he's a good guy. We need him." Rick sighed then. He didn't look confident as he walked away with his AK over his shoulder on the other side of the quarantine glass. Knowing he had his own family to care for, she wondered why he chose to stay on the outside to manage those coming in. His risk of exposure, she worried, was too great. Then again, Clarisse had no family, no one to concern herself with. But her job now was to get these people, the ones she could save, through quarantine, and it was going to take weeks with only one unit to use.

# 13

## LINCOLN

Finally able to intimidate the other drivers into getting out of his way between hacking coughs, Lincoln pulled up in a V formation right in front of a few bodies lying on the ground bleeding out on the pavement before him. "What...the...hell?" he said, looking over to the other side of the road, where he watched Officer Gance leaning against the side of his squad car, with his door open and his weapon out, balanced against the doorframe for support. It wasn't lost on Lincoln that he, too, clutched his chest, coughing and barely able to stand or see out of his watering eyes. "Damn...he's got it, too."

As Lincoln went to get out of his own unit, he noticed then that Gance was the only one standing. The other officers were either leaning back in their seats trying to breathe or he didn't see them at all.

"Come on, Enzo," Lincoln said. As he opened the door, car horns blared and between them people shouted. Gance waved to him, then wiped his eyes and swayed against the door once again.

Lincoln looked over the concrete barriers; along the highway, cars were gridlocked. People shouted at them and one another with open mouths but Lincoln could no longer distinguish between their voices. When he looked behind him...the same thing. "This is nuts."

That's when he heard Gance fire another shot above all the other noise right in front of him. He jumped, as did Enzo, which never happened. Enzo was trained for gunshots and other close encounters. Lincoln knew this one was too close to home. When he turned back, he saw a man with a child fall before him. He looked over at Gance, stunned.

Gance shrugged his shoulders.

"You didn't have to use deadly force," he shouted, though he doubted Gance even heard him.

Lincoln, distracted by movement, looked down and saw the child the man carried was a little girl, perhaps three years old, with tight blond ponytails. Wailing, she tried to sit up from underneath her father's arm. Blood covered her as it pooled from her father's chest onto the cement.

"Jesus," Lincoln said. Holding Enzo back, he reached around his car unit's door for the baby. She reached her arms up to him and he pulled her away, though it took all of his strength to do so, more than he'd expected. The sickness was weakening him already. While she screamed, clinging to him for dear life, he lifted her into the back of his squad car and closed the door. He wasn't sure if she had the virus, too. He couldn't tell through his own fever to detect hers. That's when a breeze blew through the air, the wave ruffling Enzo's fur, and when Lincoln felt it, his whole body chilled in a wave beginning from the backs of his knees up through his entire body. He shook and the hairs along his arms seemed to stand on end.

*I have to warn Paige,* he said to himself. As he looked back at Gance, he found the man now sitting in the passenger side of his unit. His arm, listlessly, still focused his rifle on the people before him. Then as Lincoln was about to sit down, everything spun around him. Stumbling sideways, he realized he might even faint.

"No, dammit."

Once seated, he detected movement on Gance's side. He was waving his arm and pointing to the far right, past the barriers.

Lincoln looked over and watched as three adults, one carrying a child on her hip, skimmed by the barriers. Lincoln looked back at Gance through the light rain that just picked up and shrugged his shoulders. "Who cares, man? Let them go. Look around you. Why the hell are we here?" That was the part he didn't understand. He'd done as ordered but after he fought his way to the front, he realized he was not only trapped there, there was no point in following those orders to begin with.

Lincoln ignored the next stream of incoherent words coming from Gance as he dialed Paige once again. It rang and as he waited for her to pick up, he looked through his rearview mirror at the toddler in the back, still wailing. Enzo watched her intently as well. "Come on, pick up, Paige," he said as he looked the child in the back seat, wondering if she also had the sickness. He couldn't tell; her mouth was wide open and her face beet red in hysterics. "Calm down, baby," he cooed. She aimed her terror at Enzo, who backed up his muzzle and looked at Lincoln with curiosity.

"She's just upset. Don't take it personally, buddy."

Then suddenly, the ringing ceased and Paige's voice mail picked up.

He ended the call. "Dammit, Paige."

That's when another wave of dizziness hit him. "God…"

He picked up his mic, feeling as if he was about to pass out. He called into the station, trying to let them know they were all down. He glanced at Gance again and the man still had one arm on his rifle, teetering now on the ledge of his opened windshield and his head hanging on his other arm. "This is Officer Asher," he said, not sure if anyone was even listening. "We need help. Officers down. I have a baby…send help—an ambulance maybe." But that was all he got out before another wave of dizziness hit him and his vision faded black from the outside. He barely noticed a blur as a few other people jumped the barrier right in front of them. Enzo barked and the baby still wailed, as his eyes closed in darkness and the world faded from view.

# 14

## PAIGE

Staring down, Paige's blue eyes examined Trevor's sport shoes. The laces on the left foot had come undone, lying in a loopy sprawl, or perhaps they were never tied to begin with when she helped him into the car early that morning; she couldn't remember. Not certain why she was doing it, she reached down and lifted both laces in her fingers and tied his laces neatly into perfect bows.

She blinked a few times then and dried the tears staining her cheeks as her head lay against his chest and unbeating heart. She lay there that way once the sobbing ceased and knew she'd fallen asleep for a time. Her eyes glanced up to the windshield, seeing that the light of day was passing her by. No longer did she hear many voices or movement past the car, stopped still in the right lane of the road.

People had honked...many drove around her shouting expletives, though she never acknowledged them as she sobbed into Trevor's lifeless side. *Again...I am crying over the death of someone I love. When will this ever end? Why do they always leave me?*

That's when she took a deep, shuddering breath, remembering her father and then her mother dying on her, too—forever abandoned by them and now the same with Trevor. She pulled her red, swollen, tear-streaked face away from Trevor's shirt. The fibers stuck to the side of her cheek when she did. Her blond hair pulled away in a stringy mass. Then she wiped away what tears remained beneath her eyes.

"I've got to get out of here," she said to herself as she sat up, purposely not looking back at Trevor's dead face...only his shoes. She never wanted her last image of him seared into her mind with his purple face, eyes bulging out. She just couldn't bear it. Instead, she looked around above his head, never looking down, out the windows to review her surroundings. A few people remained in some of the vehicles parked all over...many appeared abandoned. Some of the drivers seemed slumped over their steering wheels and others looked as they were coughing, still fighting. A couple of pedestrians staggered between the cars, trying to make their way forward. Some looked sick; some just looked frightened and kept their distance from the others. "I'm not sick," Paige said as she realized her own lungs were clear, as were few of the others she saw passing between vehicles.

"Okay," Paige said to herself, her voice breaking. She knew she'd have to leave him there and join those walking their way onward. There was no way she was going to be able to drive now through the congested lanes.

Cracking open the door, she realized it was actually cooler outside than inside her Camry. How she remained in the stifling heat of her car, she did not know. Blindly reaching back, she grabbed her purse and cell phone off the seat where they remained. She didn't look at Trevor again...she would not. She'd learned that lesson when her father died. Remember their image in death as they were in life, never the other way around. Every time she remembered her father, his lifeless body was the first thing that flashed into her mind, not the times he laughed as he pushed her on the swing or the times he puffed out his cheeks for her to deflate, ending in a grin. Never again. Trevor was not there anyway, only his body. He'd left hours before.

Closing the door behind her carefully with a crunch, Paige tentatively looked around again. Knowing her trek home would take hours and she probably would not get there before dark, she set out.

# 15

## SAM

"Addy, come on, baby. It's time to go," Sam said as he lifted his daughter's arm up. She lazily clung to him, half asleep. She was his final addition to packing that morning, and his most precious possession. Though he promised...there was one stop they had to make in the wee light dawn of day. That was the graveyard.

He would, of course, avoid all human contact but he couldn't leave her without saying goodbye. She had died only a week before, so her grave wasn't yet grassed over and wouldn't be for a time. The mounded dirt covering her casket would freeze over first, then the snows of Montana would cover that by a few feet, and finally sometime next spring tender blades of grass would emerge, winning the battle over winter as the dirt leveled out over the grave. By then, he and Addy would be long gone, alive elsewhere or dead—that was a fact Sam had to face.

Addy still...hell, *he* still, cried himself to sleep since she slipped away from them. His life was a waking nightmare, each day hoping he'd open his eyes to a new reality—that his wife had not died just recently of a long battle with breast cancer. At least they had time to say goodbye. At least they had some time to prepare Addy and yet...

no one could prepare them for the utter sense of loss he felt in his very soul. He'd only ever loved one woman in life and he still loved her in death and could not imagine loving another ever again.

Pulling his sleepy girl over his shoulder, he tightened her flannel nightgown around her bare legs. She wrapped her arms around his neck automatically and snuggled her face next to his skin so that his senses flooded with her innocent scent. His heart stayed clenched... Addy still cried every day over the loss of her mama. And knowing he was about to take Addy away from everything she'd ever known in spite of her loss...he hoped she'd sleep through their early morning drive. He'd have to explain later. Holding her close, he wrapped the blanket she clutched closely around her, still holding her warmth in the fibers. Her bare feet stuck out but he'd warmed the truck up already; she need only lie down in the back and go back to sleep. As he began to walk away from her room, he looked back quickly and spotted her bear...how could he forget? The tattered ruffian lay abandoned near the mattress' edge. Leaning over, he scooped him up and tucked the lovey into Addy's side. Then he carefully walked through the cabin he'd built with his own hands in Kalispell, Montana, seeing if there was anything else he ought to bring, then hardening, knowing everything else must stay. Their memories would remain. His boots clomped on the wood floor as he and Addy left their home for the last time.

# 16

## LINCOLN

Lincoln wiped his running eyes with the back of his hand. Even that effort cost him; they wouldn't stop watering. As he did, more people jumped the barrier. *There's no getting out of this,* he realized. Then his phone buzzed.

"Linc, you there?" Paige said as he held the phone to his ear.

"...yes. Paige...are you safe? Where are you?" he asked, trying not cough again as he held his breath.

"Linc, you sound awful. Where are you?"

"I'm...at the county border on Highway 90. Tell me where you are, Paige."

"I'm at home. Who's crying? What's that noise?"

He remembered the baby then. "Paige, are you sick at all?"

"No, I'm not. Trevor...he died, Linc."

"...Paige, I'm sorry. Are you sure you don't have it?" he asked and then heard her suppress a sob.

Just then, Enzo barked again at a group of people sliding by his unit. He took a deep breath, trying to fill his lungs with cleansing air. He'd thought about this and knew there was no other way and he had to do it before it was too late.

"Paige, listen to me...now. I need you to grab both of the go bags out of the hall closet. You know what I'm talking about, right?"

"Yes."

"Get them and come here."

"Where are you?"

"I'll send you my location; in case you lose battery, please commit it to memory. Come here, Paige. Get here as quickly as you can...even if you have to walk the whole way...it should only take you a few hours. Bring water. Do not get close to anyone, Paige. Do you understand me?"

"Yes, but Lincoln.... please...don't leave me too," she sobbed.

Taking in short breaths, he couldn't help but cough again. His eyes blurred. "Just get here as soon as you can, Brat. I love you, Paige. I need you to do something for me...it's really important," he said as he hit send on his location text to Paige and then looked again into his rearview mirror at the baby that showed no signs of the illness either, only desperation.

# 17

# CLARISSE

"Clarisse...get some sleep. Go on. I'll keep an eye on them for a while," Dalton said, nudging her by the shoulders.

She didn't care to count how many waking hours she'd spent watching over the doomed family. They all knew this was it. She kept replaying that conversation with Rick in her mind about how a few of them wouldn't make it...now, it was likely going to be more than a few...though this family would be the first she'd have to *extinguish* after their deaths. Extinguish...seemed like such a harsh word. She somehow likened the responsibility to the handler in the gas chambers of Nazi Germany. How did they do it? They were humans, after all. Though they'd wait until the last family member showed no signs of life. That was their agreement...except that it prolonged the quarantine process and others waited out there to be exposed in the meantime. There was no way around this despair.

"Clarisse...go. That's an order. I'll watch them. I'll wake you if needed."

She rose from her chair, looking through the glass at them lying there. The boy's chest still rose with each ragged breath. She checked his stats. His mother and sister had perished hours earlier and his father watched over their bodies across the room as he rocked back and forth on the opposite bed, guarding his fading son.

"He's still showing no signs. The dad might be immune. His pulse is elevated but that's likely to happen, considering."

"And the boy...how much longer do you think he has?"

Shaking her head as she slid her glasses up the bridge of her nose, she replied, "I don't know. He might even pull through. Maybe he carries some of his father's immunity? It's obvious he's fighting it. I just don't know."

Dalton nodded. "Okay, go get some rest. I'll keep an eye on them."

With one more glance back at the boy, she walked away, uncertain if she'd done all she could do for him and yet what could they do in the end but exterminate the virus in the chamber and start over?

# 18

## PAIGE

"Mom? MOM?"

Paige ducked between the stationary cars parked along the darkened highway at the shrill panic in the teenager's scream. *Oh my God,* she thought as she shook, terrified, and crouched down. Glaring headlights shone between vehicles head to tail, sending beacons of light upward between utter darkness. *How much farther, how much farther?* Paige shielded the glowing light from her phone in the void of light to check the map her brother had sent her hours before. One backpack that she didn't have slung over her back slid down her arm hard, scraping against her skin. It was heavy and she didn't wonder what might be inside, knowing whatever her brother packed in there was necessary, but it weighed so much.

"Please, please, don't die on me," she begged her phone, as her current location showed her only about a mile away from her brother. She was almost to where he said for her to go when she suddenly heard, "Stay away from me!"

"It's okay...I don't have it," a male voice yelled.

"I said stay away. I won't warn you again."

"Don't shoot! I'm just trying to pass."

"Go around then."

"I'm just trying to get by you, sweetheart."

"Don't do it. Not one more step. I know how to use this."

"Now calm down."

"Don't tell me to calm down. You could go around."

"Just listen..."

But that was all he said before Paige recoiled once again into the dark against the side of the car where she hid. She stayed there shaking, terrified to move. Not knowing who was in the right, she only heard the conversation; she didn't see the individuals. When her hearing cleared, she heard only wailing from the girl she suspected still held the gun.

*I have to get out of here.*

Stifling the sounds of her own rapid breathing, she willed herself to calm down but her pulse raced.

"Who's there?" the girl screamed again.

No one answered this time, but Paige too heard what sounded like a group of people passing by. Small chatter between the warnings of one another to keep their distance from the desperate girl.

Paige took advantage of the distraction. She placed one hand through the loop of the extra backpack and pressed her palm against the gravel on the roadway. Kneeling up on her haunches, she grabbed the padded loop and lifted it up once again, bearing the weight upon one shoulder, all the while peeking barely over the hood of the car behind which she hid to locate the girl with the gun.

The familiar gunpowder smell hung in the air, reminding her of the days her brother took her to target practice at the range as she scooted along in a crouch to the next car, her heart beating a rapid pace.

# 19

# SAM

"Where R U?"

"Outside Whitefish," Sam texted the man named Rick back.

"Specific road?"

"Hwy 93, just thru Olney."

"I C that. Just making sure the tracker is working. We may redirect u after Eureka. Know it's longer but taking u path of least resistance."

"NP, keep me updated."

"U bet. Babe okay?"

Sam looked over at Addy sleeping now in the passenger seat of his truck, having cried herself to sleep again after she woke and he explained their first stop and that they were leaving and not returning to the only home she'd ever known. It was too much for her to understand, though she took the news well.

"Yes."

"Any signs of illness so far?"

"None," Sam texted back and left it at that.

"Good."

## 20

# CLARISSE

"He's immune, Dalton. We cannot just incinerate a live human being."

"Hold on...I'm not suggesting that. I'm saying we cannot expose everyone else. How do we know he's not a carrier? The virus is alive and it's in there," he said, pointing beyond the glass.

"I'm fully aware of that," she snapped and then wiped her brow. "Look, I'm just tired. This isn't the outcome I expected."

The father had his hand on his son's chest still, though on her monitor the child was clearly flat-lined.

She shook her head. "The only thing to do is send him back out into the unquarantined zone. Incinerate the other family members and start over. Give him time to come down with it out there while we re-sterilize the unit and continue with the next family."

"What if he doesn't come down with it?" Dalton asked.

No sooner had Dalton finished his sentence when in the corner of her eye, Clarisse saw the man rise from the bed where he kept vigil over his dead son. What they hadn't noticed during their conversation was him pulling a 9mm from a concealed carry holster within his shirt.

"No!" Dalton yelled before she could register what the man was about to do. "Don't do it!"

But it was too late. He stood erect, placed the barrel of the pistol into his mouth, tilted his head straight up and pulled the trigger, falling instantly over his still son.

Clarisse heard someone screaming then, a woman's voice...later she would remember it was her own but at the time she saw only the crimson blood and gray matter sprayed over the white sterile sheets of the bed on which he lay.

# 21

# LINCOLN & PAIGE

T he child's cries intensified suddenly in the back seat, and then Lincoln caught whiffs on the warm breeze floating through the rolled-down windows. "It's okay, baby," he tried to say. She'd shit her pants and there was nothing he could do about it; as she lay in her own filth he could barely breathe through his own mouth now or see out of his watering eyes.

Enzo looked over the back seat at the girl, sniffing with his snout from the passenger side.

"I know, buddy. Paige will be here soon," he said. "She can take you both then." Without realizing it, his subconscious had already come to that acknowledgment...he was dying. He knew it. Paige and the child were not...the only thing that mattered now was his sister's survival. He had to get her out of there...the city was already nuts and she was vulnerable. She wouldn't make it in Seattle on her own.

Darting his head to the left, Lincoln knew someone was coming and Enzo was about to warn them away when he started sniffing again. It was someone Enzo was familiar with and Lincoln yelled, "Paige?" as loudly as he could through his closing throat. He'd tried to call her earlier but she didn't pick up and he'd panicked, thinking he'd put her in even more danger than she already was.

"Lincoln?"

"Paige...here," he said weakly.

Soon, Enzo was prancing in the side seat and he felt Paige's presence nearby.

She came around to him in the darkness. Enzo leaned over to sniffed at her. "Thank God. Paige, are you okay?"

"I am, but you're...sick, Lincoln."

"Yeah, I have it, sweetheart...don't get too close, Paige. Listen to me..."

"Linc," she cried and fell to her knees before he could say anything more. "Lincoln..."

"Stop, honey. You have to do something for me. Paige, listen. Stop crying. You have to take them. You have to get out of here."

"Lincoln, no. Please, please don't leave me, too."

Swallowing was impossible now. He knew what she was talking about. "Paige, I'd give anything..." but he couldn't get the rest of the words out. The coughing took him over once again.

"Take...her," he said, pointing his thumb to the back seat. "Take the girl and Enzo and go, Paige."

"Take who and go where?" She peered into the back seat through the opened window. "Who is she?"

"Needs...you, Paige. She needs you. Not sick...get her out of here."

"I cannot leave you, Lincoln. I can't leave you here."

Enzo started barking then, ferociously, to the rear of the car. Lincoln pulled his handgun, handing it to Paige. She'd always been a good shot, though she hated guns. Automatically, he watched as she crouched down in a kneeled stance, ready to fire in an instant, as he'd taught her.

"Go around," she yelled in a deep warning voice.

Lincoln had to hand it to her...she could be mean as hell, especially if she needed to protect someone. The little girl would give her that reason. A reason to move on. He hated to manipulate his little sister, but in this case, to save her, he'd play all his cards.

Whoever it was did indeed skirt their location moments later, without engagement.

"Now, Paige...You take her and go...now."

"Where? And how am I supposed to carry a little girl and everything else?"

"You'll find a way, Paige. Don't make excuses. I won't last long. You have to go. Get her out of here. Enzo, too."

"He'll never come with me, Linc. You know that."

"You have to try."

Opening the back-passenger door, Paige said, "Come here, honey." The little girl did not seem to protest with Paige's sweet voice.

"Oh my God, she smells."

"Change her," Lincoln said and found it funny, despite the awful situation, that Paige was having to deal with another human's shit at long last.

"Lincoln..." Paige said and gagged then. He would have laughed out loud if he could. He was unable to see what she was doing, but the smell got worse before he heard a thud in the nearby brush. He assumed she'd removed the girl's loaded underwear and flung it away.

"You poor thing. That's so disgusting," Paige said, "Lincoln, who does she belong to? Where do I take her?"

"Paige, listen. Map...in the pack. You take her there."

"No, I mean where do I find her parents?"

He shook his head, trying to make her understand. "Paige...you," he pointed at her chest. "You...are her parent now." And then he pointed to the dead body ahead of their position.

Paige looked horrified as she peeked over the car door with her flashlight, then sat down abruptly and whispered hard, "I can't, Lincoln. I can't take care of her."

The little girl sniffled as she stood next to Paige in the darkness. Lincoln nodded. "You're all she's got now."

Paige looked at the child as she rubbed her nose. The frightened horror he saw earlier faded away to empathy, which was a look he'd seldom seen on his little sister. "Go, Paige. Take her and go. You're both immune. You need to leave here. Follow the map in the pack. You know what I'm talking about."

She had her arm around the child then. The girl leaned into her side.

"Lincoln, I can't leave you here." Her voice cracked.

He tried to clear his throat. "I might recover. If I do, I know where to find you. Don't worry about me. We have officers coming."

"Don't lie to me."

He tried to swallow again then and nodded. She was right. He couldn't fool her. He shouldn't try.

"I love you, Paige. You have to go now."

Not saying another word, he wasn't sure how to make her leave.

She looked at the little girl again and then lifted the second backpack over her left arm and took his hand.

"Don't touch me, Paige."

"Shut up. If I don't have it now, I'm not going to get it." She brushed the hair and sweat off his forehead and kissed him. "I love you, brother." Her voice hardened in a way he'd not heard before. It was a resolve he heard...of all those who'd left her behind that she'd loved and lost. He hated that he too had broken her heart.

As she unzipped one of the packs he said, "No Paige...take it all with you."

"Shut up," she said again and took out several water bottles and put them beside him in the seat.

"Follow the map," he said.

"I know what to do. You don't need to tell me. I helped you with the packs."

Again, nodding was easier by the minute than talking. He gave Enzo a hand signal but the dog wouldn't budge.

She shook her head at him. "No Lincoln. He stays with you."

"Paige..."

"No," she demanded and took the girl by the hand, disappearing into the night without another word.

He watched as she faded from view and thought it fitting that her last word to him was no. He smiled at the darkness, sniffed and shook his head at her. His little sister...she'd just grown into an adult...right there, before him, in the last moments of his life. It was about time...

## 22

### SAM

"Addy, hurry up now. We have to go," Sam urged his daughter when he saw the headlights of a vehicle coming their way. It was one of many bathroom breaks with a little bladder aboard. He stood just on the other side of his truck with his rifle held over one shoulder by the strap. His daughter scurried just up the side of the treed embankment to do her business. She knew the routine; they'd camped and hunted on many trips. This was no different from those times, only avoiding any human contact meant life or death now. "Hurry baby," he said again, urging her to hurry up.

"Coming," she said and as she appeared through the trees, she brushed her long, tangled dark hair away from her face.

Her pure innocence never ceased to take his breath away. This child of his was made of his very soul.

Eyeballing the coming vehicle, he reached for her with his left arm, pulled her to his chest from the higher ground and then placed her immediately into the cab of the truck, locking her in as the other vehicle approached. The driver of that truck looked at Sam as he gave him the warning look in return. Diverting his eyes, the driver drove around them without breaking speed, though he gave one sharp nod as he did so. Sam caught the movement. The action was a sort of acknowledgment of the place they were in now. "I'm like you," it seemed to say. Though that once collective gesture would not matter now, not in this given moment. No one could expose his child and put her in jeopardy; he'd kill anyone that tried.

Hurrying around the side of his truck, he quickly secured himself as well, and they went on their way once again. Now that they were past Eureka, Sam expected to hear from Rick once again. Rick would detect their pit stop and want to know how things were going and just when the thought had crossed his mind, his phone buzzed again.

"Daddy? Where are we going?" Addy asked him before he could answer the phone.

"Just a second, baby, let me get this," he said as he tried to keep his eyes on the road and reply to the text message from Rick at the same time by leveraging the phone against the steering wheel.

"Potty break?"

"Y"

"You're nearing Libby...I'm directing you off of Hwy 2 after Kootenai Falls, S. There're too many guns and territory issues in Bonner's Ferry on your way to Sandpoint; instead take MT-56 S."

"OK," Sam texted back. He didn't ask questions. He knew all about Bonner's Ferry, Idaho. He had several friends there and even smiled at the thought, but he would not argue with Rick. It was best to avoid Bonner's Ferry. They did indeed have guns...lots of them.

Putting his phone down for now, he addressed Addy's question. "Sweetheart, we are headed to a safe place. I can't even tell you where it is because I don't know yet myself. It will be a surprise and we will both find out when we get there, but it's going to take some time... maybe even a day or two. Got it?"

He really didn't think she did but she nodded her head anyway. Addy was like that. She'd agree but then internalize things and he knew from experience that the wheels were turning. He'd have to be prepared for her coming questions in a few hours while she mulled this over. She was a smart girl, just like her mother...and God, how he missed her mother.

# 23

## CLARISSE

The flames she saw on the monitor told her the fire was doing the job, killing the virus by the only means they had access to so far. She'd taken blood and tissue samples, remotely, from the man who blew his brains out. He'd been the only candidate she'd had access to so far who showed immunity to the virus. That didn't mean that he might have come down with it in the near future, as they still were not sure of the virus's incubation period. There were many things they did not know about the virus still—too many unanswered questions, in fact.

When the monitor told her the heat was beginning to diminish, she knew the virus was then extinguished; what remained was the incineration of the bodies within, and that would take more time. In the meantime, since another family could not begin the process, she began working on the samples. Finding a cure for the virus was the only thing that would save them all in the end. It would be their Achilles' heel if they ran into carriers of the virus in the future. A cure was the only thing that would save them long term. She wasn't sure how to convey this vulnerability to the rest; only Dalton really knew how much jeopardy they were in. She respected the man. He seemed to understand what she was going to say before she said it and being

on the same wavelength made things easier in such dire circumstances. Never before had she realized she needed someone like him,
someone to be her person. He was taken, of course, but he made her
feel like she wasn't alone in all of this. Just his presence settled her in
a way she'd never known before.

"Clarisse?"

She jumped at his voice; she had not heard him come through the
quarantine unit doorway. "Yes?"

"There are no exceptions. You need to take a break and go eat.
Don't make me remind you. I didn't see you at breakfast or lunch
today either. Have you had anything to eat at all today?"

"I...look, I'm not used to having anyone monitor my daily calorie
consumption," she said, sliding her glasses up the bridge of her nose.

"I don't care. Get used to it. Go eat...now."

Sitting there, she stared at him. Who did he think he was? "I don't
need to go to the mess hall each time they serve food. I had coffee."

"I know, I brought it to you...this morning," he tilted his head
toward the doorway. "Go, now. I've got this."

About to argue, she watched as he rose one eyebrow at her in a
sort of challenge.

Damn him.

Huffing out a breath, she stood from her chair and walked toward
the door. As she passed him, she caught the side of his mouth tilt up
in a grin.

*Jerk...*

## 24

## PAIGE

**D**ead...*Lincoln's probably dead now,* Paige thought. *My brother's dead. Trevor's dead. My mother's dead...my father.* Her thoughts rambled through her head as she tugged the little girl along her left side and adjusted the extra backpack over her shoulder again while also tightening her sweaty grip on the Glock 19 she held in her right palm.

Knowing where she was headed, Paige also knew she'd have to stop for the night somewhere soon. Then the little girl slowed to a crawl, and the weight Paige carried suddenly felt like two anvils.

She was exhausted and with the pack, Paige couldn't carry the child as well.

*I've got to find a safe place for us to sleep through the night.*

Several headlights cascaded up like beacons in the night, even with their fading light. She'd never seen anything like it—a thick line of vehicles with stragglers wandering, yelling, sobbing in delusional hysteria or running scared. The feeling was contagious but she continued to calm her racing heart. Lincoln had taught her the biggest mistakes were made in fear. Think calmly...never panic. Panic will get you killed. Use the fear to guide you instead.

The little girl on her right side suddenly cried, pulling Paige's arm. "Keep moving forward, sweetie," she said, shaking her head at herself. *God, I sound like my brother now, too*...but she continued despite Lincoln's voice within her head. "We'll stop soon." But the girl wouldn't budge, not another step. In the ambient light of the surrounding cars, Paige glanced down at her firearm, the pack slowly rubbing her skin raw as it slid down her shoulder and the little girl in her hand.

"Deep breath...okay. Now what?"

Still on Highway 90 before Issaquah, they had a long way to go to get where they were headed. To get to where Lincoln thought they'd be safe from all of this or what might come from this. She knew he was right. The city would not be safe for a long while. They talked about what could happen, what might happen and what would probably happen...though a pandemic wasn't exactly part of the game plan. Still, he'd been right and she would follow through on her brother's plans.

For a fleeting second, she hoped. *Gotta stop that. There is no such thing as hope. He's gone, just like all the rest. It's just me now, me and this...girl.*

She knelt down then, let the pack's weight slide to the ground. "What's your name, sweetheart?"

The little girl had her finger in her mouth. She shook her head and then leaned into Paige.

Wrapping her free arm around the child, she said, "That's okay. I don't want to talk either. Too much has happened, but I have to call you something, so until you're ready to tell me your name I'll give you one. Okay?" The little girl nodded into her side.

"Um...let's call you...Franklin."

The little girl pulled away and looked up at her with big, surprised eyes. She couldn't see the color in the dark but was guessing they were brown.

"No? You don't like that one? How about...Steve? Steve's a good name. I know a lot of Steves."

The child shook her head from side to side.

"No? Don't like that one either? Christopher? Walt? Burt? Boyd? Oh wait...you're a girl. Of course, those won't do. How about Cheryl?"

She nodded then and Paige hoped she was also smiling before her in the darkness, despite what they'd both been through, but she couldn't tell, not then. "Cheryl was my best friend's name, you know. I think she would like for you to borrow it for a while." She pulled the little girl into her side for a reassuring hug then. "I know you're tired, Cheryl. I'm tired too. But you can do this...just put one foot in front of the other...keep walking. We'll find a safe place to sleep for the night and then we have a long journey ahead of us tomorrow, but I promise to keep you safe."

# 25

# SAM

The next day, and twenty-seven hours later, Sam and Addy pulled onto the North Cascades Highway after taking backroads, fire roads and even crossing a wet field in four-wheel drive, Sam gritting his teeth in hopes that his tires didn't sink into the boggy mud.

"That was fun!" Addy said, eager to try it again.

Sam let out a held breath and said, "Whew...yeah, not so much."

His phone buzzed again. "U made it! Just a few more miles."

"Ha!" Sam replied out loud. "We're almost there, honey."

A few minutes later they pulled down a long dirt road that led to another path that wasn't a road at all and continued through the dark until Sam finally made out vehicles in the distance hidden amongst the trees. "I think we're here baby," he said but when he looked over at his daughter she was sound asleep.

Which was a good thing because then he saw the armed men with face masks on, and they didn't look as if they were very friendly. Sam pulled next to one, having already been told by Rick to not open his doors or windows on approach, only to pull up and shut off his engine. Texting with Rick was his only communication. The guard looked through his window. He motioned to the girl asleep in the passenger side.

"She sick?"

Sam shook his head immediately as the flashlight shined in. He slowly reached over and shook Addy awake.

The guards were not supposed to talk to him but they seemed concerned. Addy sat up and wiped her wild hair from her eyes. "She was just sleeping," he told the man through the driver's side glass.

"No fever?" the guard asked.

"No," Sam said. "We're not sick. We weren't exposed to anyone on our way here."

He heard the guard's radio then. "Reuben...let them pass. They're the last ones. They're fine."

The guard argued into the radio mic. "The girl was lying down. I thought she might be sick. I'm just making sure they're clear, Rick."

"That's my job. Not yours. Let them in. Close the entrance now. They're the final arrivals."

"My list says there's supposed to be three here. Where's your wife?" Reuben said.

"She passed away two weeks ago," Sam said, the words still catching in his throat.

"Rick...did you hear that?"

"Reuben, I'm aware. She died of breast cancer...not the flu. Knock it off. Let them in."

Sam watched as the Reuben breathed hard. He sympathized with his internal dilemma.

Finally, the man nodded and pointed far to the right field through the forest. "Pull your truck in, far over there. Shut it off and do not exit your vehicle tonight. Sleep inside. Do you have provisions for you and the girl?"

"Yes," Sam replied.

"All right, it's late. We'll catch up with you tomorrow for more instructions. Interact with no one. I'm sorry it has to be this way for now. Until everyone is through quarantine, we have no choice."

"I completely understand."

"Welcome to the Cascade Preppers, Sam."

## 26

# CLARISSE

Staring through the glass at the new family inside the quarantine unit, Clarisse swore that they felt the presence of the last family inside. It was eerie watching them as they made their space comfortable. She reached for the intercom button. "Please make yourself comfortable and then put the monitors on the children first and then on yourselves."

The mother looked back at her with fear in her eyes. "What is it?" Clarisse asked.

"This," the woman said, holding out her hands with her palms down, "has all been sterilized, right?"

*A fine time to ask that question* was the smart answer that came to Clarisse's mind first. "Yes," Clarisse said. "Sufficiently sterilized," she repeated as the image replayed in her head when the last occupant blew his brains out and then fell over his son's body on the bed the woman now stood in front of.

"Okay," the lady said, though she was visibly shaking, and Clarisse could not blame her. No one could blame her.

Moments later Clarisse walked them through putting on the monitors and taking the first blood draws of many to come. It was such a long process but there was no way around ensuring they were not harboring the virus that would kill them all.

In the meantime, when she wasn't monitoring the family, she continued to search for a cure. And when she wasn't searching for a cure she was busy trying to avoid Dalton, who was now keeping a close on eye on her eating habits, which was driving her nuts and she wasn't exactly sure why he even cared. She'd noticed he seemed to take care of everyone in the camp in subtle ways. It wasn't just her, but she wasn't used to anyone monitoring her. She was a loner. She took care of herself. In fact, at times, she was nothing more than a ghost and she liked it that way. Only...Dalton seemed to notice this and he wouldn't let her go.

# 27

# LINCOLN

"En...zo?" Lincoln mumbled. He wasn't sure when it had happened, when Enzo leapt over him and into the open street, barking at someone or something passing too close to the squad car in the dim morning light. Enzo now licked at Lincoln's hand, something he'd been trained not to do. Barely able to breathe, Lincoln wheezed without making any effort to lift his head and through watery eyes, he looked over at where the other officer had fallen to the ground the day before. He thought he saw the body jerking back and forth in the night with an unfamiliar growling and had the horrible through that perhaps Enzo had been warding off coyotes or other dogs from the dead bodies around them, but he'd been running a fever and for the life of him, Lincoln wasn't sure if what happened was a dream or if it really had happened. He couldn't tell now, but the body was not where it had originally fallen before yesterday.

Maybe Paige would know? "Paige?" he yelled between wracking breaths. Then he remembered she'd walked away. Walked away with a little girl but not Enzo. Enzo was still by his side. His partner needed to leave. The coyotes would get him in the end. Officer Enzo never would leave his side though; Lincoln knew that. Their bond was too strong. Paige was right to leave him there. Enzo would have turned back in time. It was best she didn't bother with him.

"Enzo." Lincoln swallowed the rising phlegm that would never go away. "En...zo, go," he said and with his left arm threw out the sign to leave.

A moment later, Enzo, nudged his snout under his arm. His nose felt cold...freezing even. *Fever*...Lincoln thought and another racking cough and shivers overtook him again. "Please...go. Enzo...go," he managed to say again. The dog didn't budge. It was no use. Hopefully someone would come by and Enzo would leave and attach himself to another loyal companion. That's what Lincoln hoped for, looking down into Enzo's eyes as the dog whined at him, which was something he never did. Lincoln pulled his hand over the dog's head. "Not long now. You're the best partner and a good boy, Enzo."

*Part II - Eight Years after The Malefic Nation*

**Note from the Author:** *The Malefic Nation is where we last left Graham's Resolution. Now, we begin eight years from the past, where not only was Clarisse carrying a child, but Dalton nearly lost his life trying to get back to them, so worn when he returned that he was barely recognizable.*

*Graham is still reeling from the loss of Tala, as is the rest of the group. And not only that, Clarisse committed the ultimate crime against all of humanity to save the few who remained. With only 2% of society left and a vastly aging infrastructure to deal with, the survivors of humanity must contend now with what man has left behind and what nature throws at them or what dangers might remain on the horizon.*

*As noted in the description, The Bitter Earth ends on a cliffhanger but fear not, there is more to come in Graham's Resolution, after we've set the scene.*

# 1

## MCCANN

"Hey...no running around *in the bar*," McCann shouted as his boots clomped on the wooden floor while he carried a crate of Rick's newest brew inside the darkened building, lit only by candlelight on each table. The last thing he needed to do was to drop the coveted load, shattering the liquor all over the floor and catching the place on fire as one of the candles went careening onto the floor. Mark would kill him. Then Rick would kill him. And he was pretty sure Marcy and Macy would take turns killing him, too. But having kids underfoot was a problem. "If you can't help, at least stay out of the damn way," he yelled as the children scattered with pleasing giggles trailing out the sunlit doorway. They were obviously not afraid of him in the least.

"Why are you yelling, already?"

McCann gave Macy the eye as he sat the heavy crate on the bar. He was going to chew her out, or at least give her a hard time for not watching the neighboring kids closer, but when he laid eyes on his beautiful pregnant wife, he just didn't have the heart. Draped over her bare left arm was a damp bar towel. She raised it up to wipe the sweat from her brow again. In fact, he saw a fine sheen of sweat all along her face and neck. He cleared his throat before he spoke.

"Macy, take a break and cool off. It's not your job to keep this place clean. Just mind the bar when a customer comes in."

"It's so damn hot. It's already the end of September and the heat won't stop. Should be cooler by now."

"They used to call it an Indian Summer," he said as the beer bottles clanked together when he unloaded them from the crate and onto the leather hide covered bar.

"When do we get to go home? I'm ready to tag Mark and Marcy now. It's their turn to come back and take care of this madness. I never signed up as a barmaid. That was their deal."

After unloading the crate, he took it by one hand and let it drop down to his side. Turning to her as she held the small of her back and lowered herself down to a chair behind her, he said, "Are you sure we should make the trip back *before* you have the baby?"

"That was the plan we made. They went on vacation to Missoula for a few weeks; it's not like they're working."

"Actually, they went there to scout out new business."

"Same difference. They're at least having fun. Makes me nervous to be here too long. New people are coming in all the time. This is Mark and Marcy's world, not ours. They wanted to live here. Not me."

He took the time to choose his words carefully as he listened to the kids playing out front of the bar, their laughter floating in on the hot, dry breeze as they darted back and forth before the doorway. "It's just that you seem farther along than we thought you were."

She waved him off, the towel flung through the air, floating harmlessly to his feet. "It's just the heat. Makes me lightheaded. I don't like being here with all these people. Clarisse isn't here to monitor them for disease. I'd rather go home where it's cooler and have the baby. That's what we planned on, remember? Please say you won't change your mind."

He picked the cloth up off the floor and snapped it in the air to dislodge any sediment. "That doesn't mean we can't adjust our plans. I know you prefer to go home with the kids...and I do, too. But Macy, I'm just worried about you. What if you go into labor on the way back? It's an eight to ten hour drive these days from Coeur d'Alene,

Idaho to Cascade, Washington, with these deteriorated roads and any unforeseen complications. And there's barely anyone in between here and there. It's not like we could just pull off and get you to a hospital or call in a medevac like before the fall. At least we have a doctor here in town."

He knew better...she blew out a frustrated breath as her eyes darted at him. *Here it comes*, he thought as she waved her arm at him. *She's gonna lose it.*

"Clarisse taught you everything you know, McCann. You've treated all kinds of people around here and you've delivered a few babies in your time. Why are you so worried about attending to me if I go into labor?"

He put the crate down then, softly, on the wooden floor, took two cautious steps toward her and knelt at her side. "You know why, Macy. I was there when Tala bled out and died. I was right there." He leaned his forehead down onto her thigh. "I just can't take it when it comes to you. I was terrified when you went into labor with Ennis. Clarisse had to make me leave the room. Don't you remember that?"

Feeling her cool fingers touch the hot skin and hair on the nape of his neck always calmed him. "I remember and Ennis is fine. She's a beautiful, healthy little girl. Not a thing in the world wrong with her or me. There wasn't one complication the last time. If...something happens, I know you can take care of us. I trust in you, McCann. Please trust in yourself too."

"Hey, I can deal with most anything. I just cannot lose you."

"What the hell is going on in here? You guys are slacking...need a nap?" boomed Rick's loud voice as he walked into the saloon, interrupting their private conversation.

McCann stood up and picked up the crate. "No Rick. I'm just thinking it's best if we wait here for Macy to give birth. She disagrees."

"Imagine that...Macy disagrees," Rick said as if Macy wasn't even in the room. He leaned up against the bar, watching her.

Not surprised that Macy chose to glare back at Rick, McCann

chuckled and shook his head. "You two have always had this feud going on."

"No...she's just like another daughter to me. A bad, stubborn daughter," Rick said, crossing his arms. "But I miss her and miss seeing you guys. It was nice that you took over for Mark and Marcy these last few weeks, giving them a little vacation from here. I thought you guys were headed back this weekend anyway. Changing your minds?"

"No," Macy said abruptly. "We are not changing our minds."

"We're just discussing the options. The other problem is fire season. Hell, it's already bad and we don't have the resources to keep it under control. The best we can do is scout them out and try to steer clear. So far it hasn't been that bad along I-90, but with the warm winds here, it won't be long before it gets out of control. That's what the scouts tell me anyway. Last fire season we lost several heads of cattle and hundreds of acres of crops. All we could do was stand back and watch it burn."

"You're just trying to find reasons to stay here, McCann," Macy said with heat in her voice.

"No...no...I'm not. I want to go home as much as you do, Macy," McCann shot back.

"Wait! Wait a minute. Both of you stop," Rick said with his hands up in the air, as if trying to call a truce before their words turned into a full-fledged argument.

McCann waited for the seasoned father and husband to come out with some piece of sage wisdom while he appeared to think carefully on his next statement, but he didn't. Nothing that Rick said next helped a damn thing at all.

# 2

## BANG

As he wound down the dirt path he'd taken to the lake hundreds of times before, Bang's thoughts were interrupted by the strong scent of forest fire. He couldn't see the smoke through the trees but he could smell the strong campfire odor of pinesap boiling off in the breeze.

A barely cool, gentle wind blew past his bare hairy shins, though once he cleared the forest there was no chance of such a pleasant feel in the open. The humidity sucked the life out of you in such heat. Seeing the opening up ahead, he yelled, "Tehya?"

The flip of her fly pole was what he saw first, before her silky coal-black hair appeared.

"What?" She sounded a bit annoyed at his interruption, with an emphasis on the 't'.

"It's your turn."

"My turn for *what*?"

She knew exactly *what* he was talking about but refused to turn in his direction. "Come on, you know what."

"Why don't you ask your girlfriend?"

"Hey, you know Addy's not my girlfriend. We're just friends, and

I'd appreciate it if you stopped that. I don't do that to you," Bang said, not wanting to engage in this discussion with his little sister again.

She turned and looked at him then. He was sure it was a doubtful look but the sun glanced off the water and insects danced on the ripples. He couldn't tell what her expression was but he was sure he could imagine her doubtful gaze.

Though she wasn't really his little sister, he couldn't think of Tehya in any other way. For the last eight years he had cared for her as if she were his younger sister. They were bonded, not by blood but by family. Even though it was obvious he was Asian, she'd never asked if he really was her blood brother or not and it didn't matter, besides. In the world they grew up in now, families were made on the fly. Bonds were formed and souls were sealed. That was what happened with him and Graham, Tala, the twins and all the rest, even Sheriff. They were a family now. The past was told to the younger generation as a sort of folktale. Bang remembered little and Tehya came along at the tragic end. She asked questions about the world before but being eight years old, she only asked and was only told what was appropriate for an eight-year-old.

"Come on, Teyha, grab your tackle; it's your turn. You're not getting out of this. Don't even try."

She did as he asked but she complained as she went. "I don't see why I have to do it. They're not my kids."

Leading the way back up the trail to the cabin, Bang replied, "That doesn't matter. We've always shared responsibilities. Someday you're going to be a mother too, and you need to know how to deal with babies."

Her voice was farther than it should have been when she said, "No, are you nuts? I'm not having babies. That's where you're wrong, Bang."

He turned and looked back to see she'd stopped in her tracks on the path ten feet back, holding her pole and tack box in one straight hand, her elbows and knees locked in defiance. The baggy orange t-shirt and denim shorts contrasted with her dark skin and hair. She was a skinny, wiry little girl. Her eyes, though—her eyes were blue like Graham's. The rest of her was all her mother Tala, the mother she would never know, and she was just like her in every other way. They couldn't help but love her for that very fact.

"Tehya, come on. We need to get back. I'm not talking about this with you." In reality, he was afraid she wanted to talk about Tala and how she'd died, again. Even eight years later, he still couldn't do it. That was something he left to Graham, Clarisse, and Macy. No one else seemed to have the strength to broach the subject of Tala's life or death.

A memory flashed into his mind then, of him sitting on the bathroom counter in the cabin as Tala took care of the wounds he'd sustained from a cougar attack behind the cabin. She was a loving soul. He missed her as he missed his own mother, Hyun-Ok. He could barely remember her face now. He'd been nearly seven then, almost as old as Tehya now, when Tala died. It was old enough to make memories last and he wished they did not. He wished he'd not remembered the way things were before the people he'd loved were lost to him now. Flashing quickly on the town of Hope, across the Canadian border, right before Tala's death where she...*nope*, he couldn't let the memory in either.

Turning, with or without his stubborn little sister, Bang made his way back up the trail. She'd followed him silently though, and when they were nearly to the porch, she said, "Do you smell the burning? It's getting stronger."

"Yeah," he said, "I don't see the smoke, but it's not far enough away."

# 3

# MCCANN

"*Marriage is like a deck of cards...*
*In the beginning, all you need is two hearts and a diamond.*
*By the end, you wish you had a club and a spade.*" *– Anonymous*

LOADING the backpacks into the back of the truck with a thud, McCann said, "I cannot believe you said that. As if that helps, Rick? Remind me never to ask your advice again."

"Hey man, don't get all butthurt on me. You have to know when you're beat. Trust me, marriage is like war...it's not fair. And you picked a formidable opponent, my friend."

"Just be quiet. No more talking from you."

"Okay, fine...it wasn't one of my finer nuggets of wisdom but that's all I had at the time. In all seriousness, you guys be careful. Remember to check in every few hours. Mark and Marcy will be here in an hour or two. Sure you don't want to wait for them?"

"No, that's okay. Last thing I need is Marcy starting something with her sister and making her upset. Macy will radio along the way. She's just as mad at you as I am, so that gets me off the hook a little at least." McCann glared at him while he finished packing the pick-up truck.

"You are taking a load of free beverages back with you. You should be nicer to me. You guys are not nearly nice enough to me, considering I keep you in beer."

"Yeah, sing it to the choir, man; you know we trade for fuel. So I won't consider it a favor." His words must have come out harsher than he'd realized because he felt Rick place his hand on the back of his shoulder.

"McCann, in all seriousness, I know you're worried about her and I understand why, but...this is Macy we're talking about here. She's tough. She's smart as hell and if there was any doubt in her mind that she wouldn't make it back in time, she wouldn't take the risk. Don't you trust her instincts?"

He didn't trust her instincts because Tala was just as tough, but he loved Rick like an uncle and knew he was trying his best. "I know that Macy would make the best decisions in any circumstance, but so do I. We both have good instincts and I don't know...something doesn't feel right to me. I'm worried about her and Tala was strong as hell...it didn't matter in the end."

Nodding his head, Rick said, "I know, buddy. I get it. Now you got me worried." He ran his fingers through his oily hair, making it stand out in black shiny spikes in the mid-morning sun.

Tilting his head to one side quickly, McCann retorted, "Oh, now you're worried? Thanks. Could have used your help in there yesterday morning. Just sayin'. She pretty much berated me all night."

"Just make sure you're checking in. I'll keep a vehicle ready on standby just in case we need to get out there."

"I will. Oh look, here they come," McCann said as Macy carried out a few more things with Ennis at her side. The toddler pulled her hand out of Macy's quickly so she could navigate the three wooden stairs on her own.

"Just like her momma. Wants to do it her own damn self," Rick chuckled and when the little girl started to wobble on the last stair, McCann reached out and swooped her up and into the air and landed her into the back of the extended cab with a distracting *whee!* and giggles.

"You have to let her fall sometimes," Macy gently scolded him. "She won't learn unless you allow her to make mistakes on her own."

He held his tongue. *Nope, not gonna take the bait this time.* Rick then eyed him with a wink and a smile. Perhaps he was learning after all. Loving Macy was easy...dealing with her and her mood swings every day, not so much.

"Goodbye Rick," Macy said, giving him a quick hug and kiss. "Try to keep the bar fights to a minimum."

"Hey now, how else am I supposed to stay in shape?"

Macy waved McCann off as he offered to help her into the passenger side of the truck.

"Like mother, like daughter. Good luck," Rick said quietly to McCann before he stepped in the driver's side.

"Thanks a lot, man," McCann said and drove west out of Coeur d'Alene, Idaho.

"When are they going to fix these roads?" McCann mused to break up the silence in the cab. Macy had busied herself with getting Ennis settled down, and now they had no excuse but to talk about things.

"You say that every time. I wish it were funny still."

"Seriously though, eight years later and with the winters here freezing hard and then the spring thaw, we can't maintain what we once had."

"We don't use what we once had. There's no major semi trucks rolling down the highway."

McCann swerved slowly around a truck now a permanent part of the landscape just outside of Spokane near Ritzville. Tall native grass surrounded the rotting tires and sprang up through crevices in the shattered asphalt. "That's for sure. Besides that, fuel is still an issue, since we make our own now. Supply and demand isn't what it used to be."

"I wonder when we'll stop talking about the past. We have children now. We need to look to the future."

"Macy, I don't mean to dwell on the..."

"No, not just you. I mean all of us. That's all we've talked about for the last eight years since the fall, then the rebuild. Now the capital, if you want to call it that, is Coeur d'Alene, Idaho."

"It's more just like a major commerce hub. I don't think anyone considers it the capital. It's only because it was where people felt safe enough to gather...free of the terrorists."

"Call it what you want. It was once just a small town; now it's where everyone travels to for supplies and meeting other people. It's like a regional hub."

"Yeah, well, Seattle basically burned down. No one wants to live there anyway. That place is just a hazard zone now. Downtown Spokane is just a disaster area."

"My point is, people gravitated to one another. Some people have the need for larger cities. You and I, we don't need that. We don't want to raise our children there. We prefer the community we've created in Cascade. We're like a family."

"Macy...I just want to be anywhere you are. It's not that I don't want to raise my family there. It's just that Cascade is home. It's where most of the people are that we bonded with right after the disaster. We went through hell with one another. A damn war, in fact. It's where I met you. It's where I met Graham. Home is where you find the people you trust. You have their back and they have yours; otherwise that's no family at all. That's just a life of scavenging joy where you can get it."

"You're very philosophical this morning."

"Like you, I'm just thinking about the future. What will Ennis, and this baby, face in the next eight years? What will there be left for them then? I'm trying to anticipate what I need to teach them now."

"I don't think we can anticipate yet. We just got used to surviving the fall. Now we have to create a future with what remains."

# 4

# GRAHAM

Graham heard their steps coming up the wooden porch. Actually, he heard them coming up the trail, and their conversation as well. With opened windows, there wasn't much he missed, not anymore. It was as if, since the fall, all humans had reverted to their animalistic selves. They depended on their senses as their ancestors did to stay alive, always aware of their surroundings because their lives depended on it. The tribe depended on it and that's what they were really—a system of tribes.

"Hey guys, I just heard from Macy; they're on their way back. Should be here sometime late tonight or tomorrow."

"Oh good. Are they bringing beer?" Bang asked.

He cleared his throat. "I'm sure they are but you're still underage."

"Mark gave him one when he was here last. I saw him."

Again the throat clearing. "I know, but that was a one-time thing...right, Bang?"

"Yeah...I was, um...just testing it for him."

Graham doubted that. He knew Mark slipped Bang a few bottles here and there. So far, excessive drinking had not been a problem but he also didn't want to start on it either. There were plenty of reasons to drink. Memories alone would drive anyone alive today to want to fall into the bottle and stay there. He couldn't allow that for Bang...he wouldn't allow that for himself either.

"Okay Tehya, get going or Clarisse will have my hide. You're late, already."

The girl stomped after putting down her rod and tackle box into the corner of the cabin. "I don't wanna do this. I don't like dealing with the babies."

"We all take our turns, missy. Doesn't matter if you don't like a particular chore; you learn from it and rotate out into something you do like. That way everyone learns important skills."

"You guys are the worst. Who came up with this?"

Before he could interject, Bang intervened. "Stop your whining, Tehya, and get going."

Graham eyed Bang as he turned to him. If there was one thing he'd noticed over the years, it was that Bang seemed to know him better than he did himself some days, and he had a way of simplifying arguments and getting to the point. When Graham felt he was getting to his wits' end, Bang would always sense that and step in. The boy had become his protector and his savior since Tala's death.

Sometimes he couldn't see the strong young man with the deep voice as the little boy he once knew. Bang at sixteen was no longer the quiet, timid child he once was. Bang today was a quiet, methodical, intuitive, *don't mess with me or my family* young man.

Graham suspected in the next few years as an adult, Bang would be quite the formidable opponent. He'd already had to deal with the other boys in their community in one form or another. Some of it was the normal routine of boys growing up into manhood. It seemed each one continued to try and push Bang down from the dominant role he didn't seek or want, yet that was the role he held amongst the youth of Cascade. Graham also knew that if it weren't for his attachment to Addy, he probably would not have risen to that role. The young deaf lady had become his anchor and though Bang considered Addy a friend, Graham and the rest of the adults recognized their attachment to one another as much more than mere friendship. Much of

Bang's youth was spent keeping the girl safe from the other boys, Dalton's boys.

In time, they would see their friendship as much more, he suspected.

While he thought about their circumstances, Tehya continued to complain but was at least out the front door, and he heard her mouthing back protests as her voice dwindled into the distance by the river. She might complain the whole way, but she'd make it to Clarisse's place and do what she was told, of that he had no doubt.

Just then, Sheriff rose from the cool spot by the bunkroom door and wandered over to Graham, sitting at the table. "How you doing, old friend?"

Graham ran his hands through Sheriff's fur and massaged the flesh beneath. He looked up and found Bang watching them from inside the kitchen. With a concerned look on his face Bang asked, "How old is he now?"

"I um, I don't know, buddy. Twelve, thirteen maybe? We're not sure."

Bang emptied the glass of water he'd sipped into the sink and walked out the door.

"You're going to the gardens today?"

"Yep," Bang yelled back.

Graham watched him leave and leaned down to Sheriff, saying, "You still have some time left in you, Sheriff. We're not ready to let you go, old friend. Hang in there."

# 5

## CLARISSE

Through the window from the clinic, the young girl taking her time coming over the river's bridge reminded Clarisse so much of Tala. Even at eight the girl was her mother's doppelganger. Teyha, though, had her father's intense blue eyes and they saw right through to one's soul.

"Hi there," Clarisse said as Tehya entered the clinic. She took an exaggerated look at her watch. "You're late."

"I know," Tehya said, casting her eyes to the ground.

Clarisse smiled and said, "Come on, they're waiting for you. Can't you hear them?"

She led the way down the darkened hall of what used to, many years ago, be the quarantine building, which held so many memories, both good and bad, to the little room in the back. Lining the walls were three metal cribs, each holding a wailing infant.

When Clarisse turned to Tehya, the girl had her hands covering her ears. "Can't you make them stop?"

"I could...but that's your job. And they're crying for a reason. Any guess why they're upset? You...made them wait to be fed." Clarisse regarded her young charge and put her hands on her hips, waiting for an answer. There was nothing like natural consequences to teach a child how reality could really smack you over the head. This was a simple lesson but one that needed learning.

"Feed them," Teyha yelled over the noise.

Raising her eyebrows, Clarisse said, "Feed them what?"

"Milk...from the bottles."

"Yes, that's a good idea. You remember how to warm up the formula?"

"Yes, but you can do it, too. You don't have to wait for me."

Clarisse stood there, letting the infants protest their empty stomachs. She smiled and slid her dark-rimmed glasses up the bridge of her nose, saying nothing.

Teyha removed her hands from her ears and stalked off toward the cupboard. "All right," she said, stomping her way forward. "Did you already mix the formula?"

"Yes, we're all out of the old canned formulas so I've developed a healthier concoction. Luckily, we have a fully functioning dairy now. I don't know what we would have done if we were landed with three infants in the early days."

Teyha looked at her quietly then. "What did you do with me then?"

Why didn't she anticipate that question? "We had baby formula then." She smiled sadly at Tehya.

Clarisse watched as Teyha switched gears and first washed her hands thoroughly and then checked the chart from the first crib and then looked to the corresponding chart for the right milk bottle. She warmed the bottle up as Clarisse leaned against the doorway, observing. The baby from the first crib was old enough to turn over and pull herself up to a standing position. The baby was now in full-fledged hangry mode, her fists clenching the railings.

"I'm coming," Tehya said as she placed the bottle down on the table and, suddenly using a sweet voice, Tehya cooed, "Come on, baby, time to eat." She helped the eight-month-old lie down, placed the bottle between her hands and then propped her up to feed. Instantly, the cacophony reduced by a third. "When are we going to give them names? This Baby One, Baby Two and Baby Three thing isn't working."

"We're waiting to see if their parents show up."

Looking to Clarisse, Tehya then asked, "Can I let her hold the bottle while I get the others going? This doesn't seem fair."

Tehya looked as if she might panic. Of course, Clarisse could step in and help but then again...this was Tehya's lesson to learn. "You can, but you might risk one of them choking or soaking the bed. This is why we feed them on time."

"Fine," Tehya said. Clearly the shrieking of the other two infants bothered her. "I'm never having babies, ever," Tehya complained. "I swear, never."

Clarisse could not help but laugh out loud. "At least you'll know what you're getting yourself into when the time comes."

While Tehya worked, Clarisse stepped into her private office right around the corner in case Tehyha needed her but just out of the way enough that Tehya didn't feel like she was watching over her too much. She certainly was learning a valuable lesson today.

Taking care of the three babies that recently came into their care wasn't her call. In fact, she secretly felt the same reticent attitude as Tehya. *Not my circus.* But...they could not just leave the infants unattended and the accident that happened wasn't their fault at all. They still weren't sure where the group had come from.

Oddly enough, the two adults in the vehicle died having just escaped a forest fire near Mount Rainer—that was Sam's best hunch anyway. The SUV had sunk into a river when Sam heard the infants' cries. Why there were three babies of different parentage secured in car seats in the back seat was a mystery.

Dalton was still trying to piece together what had happened those two months ago and so far, the radio community had no answers. Three infant orphans and no one to claim them.

All three infants, two girls and one boy, were under a year old, the youngest being six months. Running tests, Clarisse determined they thankfully held antibodies to the original flu and were not at risk. In fact, they had not seen or heard of any more cases of the weaponized flu and they hoped they never would again.

Sam had only a little time to rescue the babies hastily in the rushing water and on his return, he looked downright exhausted when he came into camp. Only Addy seemed overjoyed. She loved the babies. She was also utterly deaf from her experience with the flu eight years ago, where they nearly lost her as well. So Addy was not bothered by the constant wailing of the infants either.

In fact, Addy had grown up to be a beautiful, sweet sixteen-year-old. Clarisse could hardly believe it. Though she wasn't her daughter by blood, Clarisse claimed her as her own, as she did Dalton's two sons and her own two children with Dalton since things had settled down, a boy named Logan, also nearly Tehya's age at eight, and a daughter they named Finley, now six. That was plenty to keep track of in Clarisse's mind...more than enough, actually.

The second wailing baby had quieted down as Clarisse sat at her desk. She smiled again to herself, knowing Tehya was having a day she'd not soon forget. A wailing, hungry infant was the perfect lesson of life's finer responsibility.

That's why, as a community, they came together and made the decision to share life's lessons, though they were different lessons than from their recent past. Everyone learned infant care, how to handle and maintain a firearm, how to make a bow and arrow that would penetrate flesh and provide meat for the table, water purification, shelter construction, how to secure a perimeter and deal with strangers, who endured days of surveillance before they were ever allowed to approach camp. Those were just a fraction of the many new life lessons to learn, and they never stopped learning or evolving.

Just when the third infant finally settled down, Clarisse heard the front door open and Dalton's familiar footfalls came her way down the hall. When he rounded the corner he said, "Hey, guess what?"

"What?"

He screwed up the side of his face and said, "Sam found another one."

"What?" Clarisse said and stood up from her desk as her jaw dropped. "Another baby?"

Tehya yelled from the next room, "No more babies!"

Dalton chuckled at the outburst and looked a little confused. "Well, this one's not an infant exactly. She's actually around ten or eleven. Sam radioed in and said he found her wandering a dirt road with burns on her hands and feet. Says her name is Cheryl."

# 6

## MCCANN

Soon after they crossed the wide expanse of the gorge after George, Washington, McCann remarked, "Damn, is it me or is the smoke getting thicker in the distance?"

No answer came from Macy and when he looked over, she was sound asleep with her head against the window. Glancing in the rearview mirror, he found his daughter Ennis also asleep, softly snoring, her fat baby cheeks flushed from heat and her long eyelashes standing out against her pale skin. It would have brought him contentment but the hazy view in front didn't allow for that. They were entering a wide-open expanse of land, no trees visible until they hit the outskirts of Wenatchee, near the Cascade Mountain Range and yet, the smoke was thick as the L. A. city fog before the fall, which meant there was one hell of a fire up ahead.

Pulling out his radio, McCann called in. "Any reports of fire near the mountain range? Any redirects?"

Rick responded, "Um...not as far as I know, but it's been iffy lately. Of course, I no longer have a satellite link up there. I can't tell you for sure. How's the wind speed?"

"It's coming in northeast at about ten to fifteen. Not too bad, normal really, but it's blowing a ton of smoke this way. If I get any closer and lose visibility in the mountain pass...this is going to be a problem. I think I should redirect north now, while we're right outside of Ellensburg."

Rick shuffled what sounded like a paper map to McCann's ears. Gone were the days of tracking by satellite. Old school navigation was now the norm. "Yeah...you'll have to go north on 97 up to Leavenworth, but that's a pretty dense forest and we don't know where the fire is coming from. That's a risk because you're forced alone onto a tiny winding roadway with limited escape options. Let me do a radio fire forecast up ahead and see what's going on. Just hang tight. I'd rather not divert you there unless necessary. The old-timers on the radio keep warning about the Great Fire of 1910."

"Okay, I'll standby."

While Rick did some checking, McCann slowed to a stop in the middle of Highway 90 and turned off the engine. There was no need to expect anyone to come along. No one ever did. Ellensburg was once a midrange city right in the middle of Washington State but as the population drastically dwindled, if there was anyone in town, they kept out of sight. The view was crystal clear on most days, directly to Mount Rainer in the summer months and the Cascade Mountain Range, but not today. He barely saw over the ridge.

From his front shirt pocket he pulled out a toothpick, patting the thin cotton material to take a cursory count of the supply that remained, and placed the tiny stick in the side of his mouth. Chewing on the wood calmed his nerves and anytime they scavenged houses, boxes of toothpicks were always welcome luxuries. If his supply ran low and none were found, he'd been known to whittle his own. And once, Macy even made a few for him during a long drought of not finding the blasted things. She was an enabler to his bad habit, but at least he didn't smoke or drink excessively. One didn't survive long with such vices, not in this world. Dependency, on anything, wasn't wise in the post apocalypse. Though many did try to numb the past only to jeopardize their future.

That is, except for adult beverages...coffee was a human necessity. That was a fact. They had to do without things for very long stretches at a time. It was always best to become adaptable, without dependencies. Now that trade had picked up once again, java was still a hot commodity and few did without. That and beer, now that Rick had cornered the market on the growing of hops and the fine art of brewing. Mark and Marcy owned and managed the taverns and beer distribution.

Smokers in the north seemed out of luck. Tobacco had yet to make permanent strides in a market in the northern United States. Though in the South, it was a growing commodity, as it was at the nation's birth. McCann hoped they kept that stuff down there because instead of a stick in his mouth, he was afraid he'd pick up the habit as an exciting placeholder for the coveted toothpicks.

"What's going on? Why are we stopped?" Macy asked in a drowsy voice.

"Because of that." McCann pointed out the front windshield and if he didn't know better, he would've sworn the smell of forest fire was even worse than a few minutes ago and the wind was picking up.

"That doesn't look good."

"Nope."

"What did Rick say..."

But she didn't finish. Rick's voice crackled over the radio just then. "You guys are going to need to bail."

"What?" Macy asked in an agitated voice.

"Come again?" McCann asked into the mic.

"I mean it. Turn around, come back. It's not safe to go any farther."

Macy raised one eyebrow. "Did you put him up to this?"

"Are you kidding me? Macy, look ahead." McCann pointed ahead. "No, just no. I'm not capable of planting a massive forest fire in our path just to persuade you to give up on this trip."

"No, but..."

"Turn around, you guys..." Rick's voice faded as McCann restarted the engine, while the wind picked up enough to blow tumbleweeds over the worn highway, followed by thickening smoke.

# 7

## GRAHAM

Not long after Bang left for the community garden, Graham felt a dry breeze seep through the screened window and on that breeze, he smelled forest fire.

Even Sheriff seemed alarmed by the ominous message riding the wind. "Getting worse I suspect." Graham walked outside of the cabin, allowing the screen door to slam on its own accord after Sheriff walked through, too. Not only did he smell fire on the wind, he saw the thick light gray haze beyond the tall pines in the far beyond.

They'd dealt with forest fires every year since they ran unabated at nature's whim, though so far, the people of Graham's camp had yet to evacuate from the dangers, though always, they were prepared.

Just as he was about to return to the cabin to radio in to Dalton, he saw the man coming his way with his customary limp. Hell, they all limped in one way or another from past injuries, working too hard or just plain mental fatigue. Dalton was lucky to be alive after his unlikely return. The man had not only survived the pandemic, he survived a bear attack, countless firefights, starvation on the long road home, and Clarisse. He was a true legend now, and a lifelong friend.

"Hey, I was just going to call in. Who ordered the fire?"

"Ha, lame joke, Graham."

"Yeah, well...that's all I've got these days."

"That's why I came, actually. Rick radioed in, said there are reports of a massive fire in the Wenatchee forest that jumped I-90 and now it's taking over the Cascades, according to a few scouts. We can't really confirm the sightings but no doubt there's something on the way," Dalton said, jutting his chin out quickly to the haze in the distance.

"Well, that's southwest of us and the wind is blowing south. Are we in the direct path?"

"We're on standby for now. The wind could change. That and Rick had Macy and McCann turn around in Ellensburg. It's too risky to drive through the pass right now."

"Oh hell, yeah, they can't go through that. I bet Macy was pissed."

Dalton just chuckled. "We need to get things ready if we need to evac."

"No problem."

Trees began to sway in the unusually dry breeze in the Pacific Northwest, which caught Graham's attention. "That smell and the brittle tinder...seems like a bad sign. It's usually moist here this time of year; we're not used to this. We didn't have much of a snowpack last winter. I guess that means we're in trouble this fire season."

When he looked back at Dalton for a response, he found his friend not looking at the swaying tree line in the distance; rather, he was looking at Sheriff. And Graham had come to know the many faces of Dalton over the years. He was concerned but not stating the obvious.

"Yeah," Dalton finally said, still holding his gaze on the beloved dog. "I agree. I don't remember it ever being like this in the fall, even during fire season when we were kids. Even in long summers here, it's always damp, even for days without rain."

Dalton finally met Graham's gaze, not mentioning Sheriff and what Graham knew was on everyone's minds lately.

"No, me either," he said. "Oh, and Sam found another straggler."

"Not another baby?"

Dalton laughed as if not understanding what all the fuss with babies was over.

Graham knew Dalton actually liked the babies.

"No, a young girl. He's bringing her in tonight. She's about Teyha's age, a little older maybe. She's got some burns on her hands and feet and she seems shaken up," he said.

Graham just nodded. He was thinking what Dalton was probably hinting at, that it might be good for Tehya to have a companion her own age here. That they had room for another person and that the girl could live with them, since a few of his had grown up and moved on already.

"We'll have to mend her wounds first but consider taking her in with you guys."

"I know what you're saying. Let's just see how things work out first. We haven't even met her yet."

"I know what you mean. There was a time you took in kids left and right, though. Now that's changed."

"Let's just say I'm old and tired now."

"Or more likely, wiser heading into our Golden Years," Dalton laughed as he turned and walked back to his side of the Skagit River.

## 8

# SAM

Every few weeks, Sam felt like he had to get out of the camp. He often volunteered to bootleg Rick's brew from one region to another while also trading fuel for other needed items. It wasn't really bootlegging because there were no other distributors, but he liked to think of himself as a bootlegger all the same. Truth was, he was also a scavenger of useful things.

Getting out of camp for a few days was great but for the second trip in a row, he kept stumbling upon orphans, and that was getting old. The last time he was out, he had Addy with him when they came across the three infants.

On their second day on the road, he'd come across a Suburban half submerged in a river, just barely floating downstream in the rushing waters. He'd just crossed the bridge and dammit if he didn't hear a baby crying. He followed the river until he found the vehicle again, only this time it was stuck in the middle of a sandbar of quickly flowing water. Addy quickly started signing she'd seen movement in the back seat. He could not have stopped his teen daughter from jumping out of the truck before he came to a complete stop if her life depended on it.

Throwing the vehicle into park, he jumped out and ran in front of her to keep her from jumping into the water before him. "Addy, no!" he'd yelled, fully aware that she would not hear a damn thing he said, but she would see his expression and she could read his lips.

Pulling her away from the water's edge, he handed his rifle to her and said, "Stay right here. Cover me and watch the vehicle." It was just easier to let her read his lips rather than sign his every intent, though he knew she could probably guess his every move with no communication at all.

She'd spun around to view their vehicle and back at him, finally understanding it could be some kind of trick at stealing their stuff, a diversionary tactic they trained against. Nodding then, he crept out into the rushing river. The sounds of a baby's cry increased the closer he came to the vehicle. "Hello? Hey?" he yelled, hoping to get the attention of the adult clearly slumped over the steering wheel in the front seat but when he got there, all he saw was blood. The windshield was shattered by what he suspected were bullet holes. When he looked in the back seat, he saw not one baby, but three of them, all screaming at the tops of their lungs as they were strapped into car seats three across. Another person, wearing a mint green t-shirt splotched with dried red blood, was slumped over in the front passenger seat. They'd been dead for a while.

Pulling his Glock 19 from the back holster of his pants, Sam held it up and glanced back at Addy. Everything appeared okay ashore, but the hair rose in a follicular ovation along his arms and the back of his neck, and it wasn't the icy water raging past his knees. This was murder. These people were fleeing for their lives and died trying to get away. He looked around then. Seeing no other threats, Sam reached in and checked the neck pulse on the driver, finding it absent. The water was rising in the vehicle and then the whole thing began to shift forward slightly.

"Daddah!" Addy yelled out in her distinctive voice.

He held his hand up. "I'm okay," he yelled back.

There was little time then; he had to get the babies out of the vehicle before the suburban floated away with them in it and out of reach. He quickly reholstered his weapon; he'd need two hands for this, and quick. This might be his only chance to save them. The driver was dead with at least one gunshot wound to the chest or face —he didn't have time to investigate—and he suspected the passenger was the same. His priority at that moment was to save the lives of the wailing infants.

With the window glass shattered, all he had to do was reach in and open the back seat door quickly. There was no way he was going to pull Addy into the raging river to help in the rescue operation, putting her at risk as well.

Opening the door, he quickly released the first infant from the car seat harness, pulled the baby out and flung him, or her, over his forearm. He did the same with the second infant. With the third, though, he felt the Suburban's weight beginning to shift again, and just in time, he released the latch on the car seat. He was only able to grasp the edge before the weight of the vehicle began to slide. He gripped with all his strength, holding two infants in his left arm, and hauled the loaded car seat out with his right arm...and then, the vehicle and its two dead passengers floated away downstream. He watched for a split second before he had to jerk down and get a better handle on the flailing infants or risk losing them in the river.

There was nothing he could do with his arms full but watch the vehicle float away and try to get back to shore with three wailing infants, who he soon found out smelled beyond horrible.

Remembering that scene just a few weeks ago, he shook his head as he did then and during the insane ride back into camp in the single cab of his pickup truck. Though Addy seemed to love the babies, he couldn't wait to hand them over to Clarisse. She would know what to do with them. He remembered just putting the truck in park and getting out. Walking straight to the old quarantine building, he just knocked and when Clarisse came to the door, he could only point to his truck. His beaming daughter and the intense wailing coming from within answered Clarisse's many questions.

Once the babies were taken care of, Sam relayed the condition of the driver and adult passenger to Dalton. Unfortunately, the vehicle was washed away and there was no way to find out what exactly happened to them. Initially, Sam swore the shattered window and wounds had to be the result of gunshots, but now, thinking back, he wasn't so sure. "Maybe it was an accident?" Dalton had asked. "Perhaps the driver swerved away from a deer, hit his head on the windshield and then the vehicle ran into the river? I don't know."

They'd never know the play of events with only three infants as witnesses. Dalton continued to relay the information out over the radio waves but it seemed, after a few weeks, no one knew a thing. People kept to themselves for the most part, if they had a community to depend on. It wasn't out of the normal range of thinking, in this closed off society, that babies could go missing and no one would report them except those in their own community.

Now he was out again, making another beer supply run for Rick, when suddenly he saw this girl just stumbling down the middle of a road, wearing no shoes. He pulled over to the side and watched her, thinking someone was certainly close by, though after a time, no one showed up and not only that, the girl looked as if she was about to collapse from sheer exhaustion. She was around Tehya's age, if he had to guess, scrawny and malnourished, which wasn't unusual post-collapse, but this girl looked like she might even pass out and just as the thought crossed his mind, she hit the dirt path only thirty yards from him. He waited a little longer to observe if anyone came to her aid. Nothing. So he opened his vehicle door and cautiously walked in the girl's direction. "Hey, young lady. Are you okay?"

At his voice she moved her knee, barely, in response to protect herself. He'd seen the defensive posture too many times to count, but he was really looking into the forest for any sign of movement. He rarely came across anyone wanting to rip them off anymore. The survivors these days were typically made from sturdy stock. They'd all been through so much that thieves by now were extinct for good reason. However, he was always cautious and expected anything in compromised moments. There was always a first. So far, after the fall, folks were just happy to meet others, engage in trade and engage in general storytelling of their experiences.

"Miss...are you all right?" he asked again once he came upon her body lying there on the hot dirt road. Obviously, she was not all right. Her eyes were open and dull; she moved the back of her hand to her mouth the way a child will do in fear. Her knees drew farther up but she seemed drained of energy with this effort. Her chest, however, began heaving up and down.

"It's okay, baby. I'm not going to hurt you."

He looked around again and saw no one lurking. Relatively sure the girl was on her own, he knelt down cautiously and noted her bloody, cut-up and bare feet, and then he saw the blistered insides of both her hands.

"Hey, looks like you've come a long way," he said and then she lost it and began crying, though she seemed to strain even for tears. Hell, he would have cried too, walking on the burned soles of her feet. "Come on, darlin'," he said and slung his rifle over his shoulder and froze for a half second, taking a last cursory look at his surroundings before scooping up her too-thin body. If someone was going to jump him, now was that time. He even paused again once he had her in his arms in preparation for an attack, and still nothing happened.

Once he got her into his truck, he gave her his thermos of water and applied salve to her feet and hands, then wrapped them up in his spare clean t-shirts. "Can I bring you to your people? Do you know where you live?"

She shook her head. "No, they're gone. The fire and the bad men came." And she began sobbing again.

"Okay, okay, calm down now. Can you tell me what your name is?"

She sniffed and looked at him, her eyes now glossy from tears. "Cheryl," she said between hiccups.

"Crap," Sam said under his breath once he got her settled down and radioed in to Dalton again for the second time in a month that he was bringing in yet another orphaned child. They were starting to make fun of him in camp now every time he brought in another addition, and he didn't like it one bit.

# 9

# RICK

*Z*oning out in the glossy lantern light reflecting on the bar, Rick put down the radio again as he heard a familiar pickup truck roll up the gravel driveway out in front of the bar. Music blared, so he knew exactly who it was then. He wasn't expecting McCann and Macy for at least another hour and they were expected to arrive in a very bad mood when they did, if he knew Macy at all.

No, this truck's signature sound belonged to Mark and Marcy. They came in from the opposite direction, having made the trip to Missoula. And he hoped they were successful at obtaining new business. The problem was, he always tried to avoid having the twin sisters' visits at the same time. They were fine when they were apart, but fought like beasts when they were together for more than a few days at a time. The limit was three days, tops, he decided. Unfortunately, this time the situation could not be averted. They'd all have to deal with them and the fallout that would inevitably arise from prolonged exposure.

Besides that, last time he heard about the Missoula settlement, they were heading toward a more cultist society, letting no one in or out who didn't have the right affiliation with God. They weren't exactly zealots; they merely required a faith to enter. That was *no bueno* as far as Rick was concerned but his question now was...do they like beer? That was the question and that's also why he and Mark devised a visit just to see if they were possibly open to the idea. Rick had heard only cursory reports from Mark because they assumed, like they always did, that their conversations were monitored. OPSEC was forever a worry, and a wise decision that was, too.

"Hey old man."

"Knock that off right now, Markus," Rick said. "Welcome back, moron." He hugged Mark like a son. Doing so was their way; you cherished those you went through hell with as family.

"And you...Macy's sister...how was the trip?"

"Is that what you call me now? I'm not worthy of my own name?"

"It depends."

"Depends on what?" Marcy asked, eyeing him as she let her baggage slump down onto the barstool next to her. Her hair was braided down one side of her shoulder. It was as if the girl always tried to make herself physically distinguishable from her twin, an effect she seldom achieved but kept trying for even into adulthood. If Macy had a child, Marcy proclaimed she was never having children and so far, that proclamation had proven true.

"If you guys were able to get a distribution agreement with the Missoula tribe." *She is not going to like my next news, so I'm going to piss her off now,* he thought.

"You're in luck, old man," Marcy said with a smile.

"Watch it there, missy."

Mark interrupted, his hands in the air. "My news to tell...Yes, we have a contract with a bar owner. Seems the Missoula tribe does indeed have a taste for the brew. They have a small operation, but nothing like ours. We can begin shipments in a few weeks. But I tell you...that's a long, harrowing trip. Fourth of July pass is a bear. We were in a pickup truck, not hauling heavy loads of supplies. I think we're going to have to do some road repairs before we get too serious, and there's no way we're making that trip over Look Out Pass in the winter. Not if it's anything like last winter."

"Yeah, I was afraid of that," Rick said.

"They have nice hotels there, though," Marcy said. "It's like living in the Old West. Dances and prayer meetings and stuff. I liked it there."

"Hmm," Rick said. "They had those in Nazi Germany, too. People do like a good get-together."

"Pfftt, it wasn't like that at all," Marcy said.

Rick stopped and just looked at Mark, who had his eyebrows raised to the ceiling but said nothing.

"Yeah...I'm sure you're right. Tell me something—was there anything that made you uncomfortable? Anything unusual?"

Mark shook his head. "Nah, nothing like that. Everyone's armed. There's no swastikas or anything...if that's what you're getting at."

"That's exactly what I'm getting at. You know how it goes: one man's apocalypse is another man's perverse utopia. We've come across that before," Rick said. He picked a few things off the bar to take into the back, and said over his shoulder as he retreated into the back room, "And by the way, McCann and Macy will be here in about an hour. They had to turn back." He caught Mark's eye roll before he turned away and quickly left the room so he could deal with Macy's sister.

# 10

# CLARISSE

s Sam carried the young girl into the infirmary, not long
after Dalton announced the incoming patient, Clarisse had
an exam room ready for her. "Set her down here, Sam,"
Clarisse said.

The little girl shivered even through the unseasonably warm
conditions. Clarisse checked her temperature but suspected the
tremors were the result of fear more than anything else. The ther-
mometer beeped and confirmed her suspicion. "Sweetheart, you're in
a safe place," Clarisse said and gave the girl a gentle hug. "No one is
going to harm you here. Can you tell me your name?" Already aware
the girl's name was Cheryl, Clarisse watched the girl's speech and
tested her eyes while she answered. Her cognitive responses seemed
fine.

"Cheryl," the girl said.

"Do you have a last name?"

She shook her head, indicating that she either did not have one or
did not know what it was.

"Okay, let's take a look at those burns then, shall we?"

But when Clarisse went to unwrap the cloth around the girl's
hands, she retracted into Sam's side.

"Would you prefer that Sam help you take those off?" Clarisse said.

And instead of saying so, the girl only nodded.

Clarisse smiled up at Sam, as if saying, *You've got a friend.*

Without Cheryl seeing his reaction, he rolled his eyes but comforted the child all the same.

Clarisse went into the next room for first-aid supplies while he calmly talked Cheryl through peeling off the wraps on her wounds. She heard him murmuring things like, "See, it's not so bad. Better to let the air get to the wounds. The more they dry out, the faster they'll heal."

Sam was quite caring when he needed to be. He was a wonderful father to Addy, and Clarisse thought it might not be such a bad idea for Sam to have a new apprentice now that Addy was growing up. It was an idea if no other family unit presented itself. Perhaps this young girl might bond with him instead of Graham's camp...time would tell. These things had to happen naturally. Any forcing of these bonds, they discovered over time, only resulted in failure. The three babies in the next room were up for grabs still. They'd yet to even think of discussing which families they might go to in hopes that their original families or communities might come forward.

So far, there was no luck and Dalton had spent extensive time with the radio network to get the word out. If nothing else worked they might bring them to Rick in Coeur d'Alene, Idaho since that community was much larger and could absorb three infants more readily. Though for now no decisions were made about the babies' futures.

As Clarisse entered the exam room once again, Sam was carefully peeling off the last of the bandages that stuck to the blistered wound on Cheryl's inner right sole. "See, that wasn't so bad," he said.

But they all knew the wounds were very painful. Anyone with the same conditions would argue how bad the pain was. Clarisse gave her a cup with two anti-inflammatories and a chaser of water. That would help cut the pain and inflammation at least.

"What you need after I get you patched up is a good meal and some sleep. Then maybe you can answer some questions for us, so we can help you find your people. Does that sound all right?"

Cheryl nodded with a weary expression. She looked as if she had not slept in days and the prospect of having a meal and sleep in a safe place probably made her want to pass out right there.

"Sam, could you get Cheryl something to eat? Something mild. I'm not sure what we're serving today. The anti-inflammatory won't settle well on an empty stomach."

Cheryl clenched Sam's shirt, but he peeled away from her fingers while saying, "Clarisse is the best person I know here. You're in great hands with her. I would never leave you with anyone I didn't trust."

Cheryl's wide brown eyes turned to Clarisse in acceptance.

"You're safe here. I promise," Clarisse said while brushing the child's unruly, matted hair with her hands.

Knowing that cleaning out the blistered wounds on her hands and feet would cause the girl tremendous pain no matter how gentle she was, Clarisse began asking the girl questions to get her mind off the task. "Can you tell me how you were hurt? How did this happen?"

So far, she'd only said her name and when the girl began to speak, her voice came out with a terrified tremble as she recalled her escape from the deadly fire and the separation from her mom.

The tale was so harrowing that when Sam returned with a tray, Clarisse met him at the doorway and, finding herself shaking, she whispered, "Get Dalton down here now. I'm going to have to sedate her soon, but he needs to hear this." Shaking her head as if she didn't want to believe what she'd just heard, she added, "Maybe we didn't get them all, after all."

# 11

# MCCANN

As soon as McCann pulled up to the bar in Coeur d'Alene, he spotted Mark's truck on the crowded street before Macy did and let out an unprepared groan. By midafternoon local customers had found reason enough to float in and out and in again, partaking of their favorite beverage.

"What?" Macy said suddenly, raising her head to see what he groaned about. "Oh, Mark and Marcy are here? What's wrong with that? It is their bar."

"Oh, nothing," he said and avoided any further discussion by exiting the truck and pulled out their luggage as Macy retrieved Ennis.

"I swear we just left this place," Macy said as she helped her daughter up the stairs again.

McCann held the door open for his family as Mark came over and helped with their bags. Both men watched as the two sisters greeted one another amongst the customers enjoying their own company. This was always their way. Niceties for a few days and then they fought like cats and dogs for any longer than that. McCann gave a knowing look to Mark as he smiled, his eyes wide. "Nice to see you, bro," Mark said and McCann gave his adopted brother a pat on the back.

Then Mark claimed little Ennis from the floor and twirled her around, exclaiming how tall she'd grown since the last time he'd seen her.

"When are you guys going to start a family?" Macy asked her sister as they followed Mark to the back rooms, and suddenly McCann thought, *Oh hell, here we go already.*

Surprisingly, Marcy replied, "We're taking our time. No rush. Did you know we just got back from Missoula?"

"Yes. We had to turn around before Wenatchee. The fires are pretty bad, we hear," Macy said.

Mark still held a smiling Ennis as he said, "How's Graham's camp? Are they on evac notice?"

McCann thought Mark would know more than they did at this point but Rick wasn't in the bar at the time of their arrival, so he wasn't sure of the latest news.

"Got me. I take my orders from Rick. Where is he anyway?"

"He went back to his place at the hops farm to manage the radio. We were just cleaning things up in here. This is my bar, you know."

"Yes, we know; that's why the sign outside says Mark's Bar."

Macy said, "Yes, that was very original of you."

"And did you know I'm the only Mark in town?" Mark said.

"Still?" Macy said. "There must be two hundred people here now."

"The one and only. When I was a boy in grade school, I was always one of three Marks in my classroom," Mark said and Ennis giggled.

"That, I believe," Macy replied.

That's when pounding footsteps came running up the back path. McCann wasn't surprised when Rick bolted through the back door, looking mad as hell, and said, "We've got problems."

# 12

## GRAHAM

"What in the hell are you talking about?" Graham said as Dalton explained what they'd learned from the ten-year-old girl Sam found and brought into camp.

"These fires...they're being set...on purpose," Dalton said, nearly out of breath.

"By whom? Look, we have a fire season every year. We had very little snowpack this winter; a larger fire season was bound to happen this year."

Dalton shook his head. "This is not only a tough fire season. We're not completely sure. She's only a scared ten-year-old girl. She says—her words, not mine—that the bad men wearing black took over their place, cutting the heads off all the men in their camp. They took all the women and the children. She said her mother helped her escape while they were being transported. She said the men were setting fires as they went."

"No, Dalton. Don't overreact. We killed them. We killed them all."

"What if, and we've talked about this scenario, what if more arrived? It's been eight years, Graham. There's been enough time for them to regroup and plan another attack."

"What about the radio network? We would have heard something. You said she was scared. Maybe she's delusional too? Don't look at me like that. We need to verify her story before we go crazy, don't you think?"

Dalton rubbed his hand over the stubble on his chin. "Maybe you're right, Graham, but do you really want to take that chance? I don't want to give them ground. It doesn't really matter; we're going to have to evacuate soon because of the fires anyway. They're headed this way. We leave in the morning, and we have to keep watch as we do. Flushing out a community with fire would be an ideal way to catch them by surprise."

"Don't you think we need to keep this information to ourselves for now? We don't need to scare the hell out of the kids over this."

"Graham, the twins, Mark and McCann already know. There's no keeping Rick's mouth shut."

"That's all right but Bang was just a little kid when all this happened. Your guys...I don't think they really even remember much of the war then. To them, this has all been an extended camping trip after the pandemic. Let's focus on the imminent threat, the fire, but keep the rest to ourselves until we know for sure."

"You're forgetting my boys, Kade and Hunter, lost their mother during that time. I don't disagree, Graham, but once verified we have to get the next generation ready. There's a chance there were a few immune just like you were, or a new wave of Islamic terrorists bent on jihad are still after us."

"Or this is just a normal fire season."

More needed saying but at that moment, Bang came through the door with Tehya beside him. Bang stopped short and Tehya nearly ran into his back. The young man knew something was up. He was always the perceptive one. Graham knew Bang could sense tension in the air.

"Hey guys," Graham said as Sheriff ambled over to greet them.

The sun had just dipped completely below the horizon. Crickets chirped in the night and as Graham waved goodbye to Dalton, a dim glow from a faraway blaze could be seen over the distant southern tree line. Without a breeze, a cold chill ran up Graham's spine.

## 13

# RICK

"The fires are being set on purpose. Seems we have an arsonist or worse on our hands," Rick said.

McCann stepped forward. "An arsonist?"

Rick put his hands up, trying to calm his racing heart before he spoke more. "Sam picked up a stray girl in pretty bad shape. She said there were bad men who ran into their community and beheaded all the men, taking the rest captive. She escaped somehow. She said they started the fires and then captured them as they tried to run."

"Sounds like more than just arsonists," McCann said.

The last thing Rick wanted to do was scare them. He had no choice, though. This was their reality. They weren't kids anymore; they were full-fledged adults. They were the leaders. He wouldn't sugarcoat things, not even for Macy or his own daughter Bethany, who was now a mom of her own.

"McCann, I've heard from three different stations now. They've got some crazy tales of unknown watercraft coming to shore. Bellingham, Bremerton, and a community near Portland. At first they said there were ships coming up the sound, but I thought it was probably someone starting a fishing business or something. No one really confirmed the sightings after that. Several of the other communities don't even check in on their daily roll call. That's not like them. Occasionally maybe—we've all become a little lax. I assumed at first it was because of the fires. They evacuated and didn't relay the information." He shook his head. "We've gotten too complacent, but not that lax. I think...I think they've been taken over. If this girl's story is true, and I think we have to take this threat seriously now, they're back."

"Who's back?" Marcy asked.

"The terrorists," Rick said.

"The terrorists? What do we do?" Macy asked.

"How did we get rid of them the last time?" Marcy asked.

That's when Rick realized these guys really didn't remember, or perhaps they never knew of the controversial way they eventually defeated the terrorists the last time around. Or in some circumstances, the brain shuts down memories too terrible to remember. It could be that as well. McCann knew.

"We gave them a taste of their own medicine," McCann said. "It was the only way then. Rick, did the radio network ever mention how many men were aboard the boats? Did they come ashore? What they looked like? Any of that information relayed?"

"No, not really. They only reported seeing unusual boats in the harbors."

"Are there any reports of them arriving anywhere else aside from the west coast?"

"I put the word out, but I've not yet heard back."

McCann nodded but he was red in the face by then. Rick saw the pending doom rising up through the young man, watched him look over at his pregnant wife's baby bump, and little girl, Ennis, in her uncle's arms. Instantly, he went from a responsible husband and father to a soldier, a murderer, a madman willing to do anything to save his family from a recurring nightmare, to end it once and for all.

*Good*, Rick thought, *because that is what's needed now.* He'd been there before himself. He knew what it would take. And he would do it again, if this turned out to be what he suspected it was—and he had no hope that it was some kind of misunderstanding or humanitarian aid coming their way. Or a new fishing venture. Beer was one thing, but he suspected sushi wasn't going to make it this far inland ever again.

"What do we do, Rick?" Mark asked suddenly, as if the danger had just hit him.

"We lock down. Call in the town, shut down the highway, and get ready."

"What about Graham's camp? We can't just leave them out there," Macy said.

They all looked at one another for the longest split second.

"Macy, they're on their way here. They're a part of our tribe. They'll be fine," Rick said, but he wasn't sure. He had to give her hope, even when he was afraid there was none to give if the circumstances were what he suspected. They weren't safe. None of them were safe.

## 14

# GRAHAM

The next morning came well before dawn and with an even stronger aroma of a forest fire on the breeze. Actually, Graham slept very little during the night. Tehya went to sleep rather early after dinner. She seemed exhausted after her day with the babies, and she'd even complained in her sleep, saying things like, "Quiet, babies!"

He'd told both Bang and Tehya their plans to evacuate in the morning, as a precaution due to the coming fire danger, but after Teyha yawned and he'd sent her to bed, he told Bang the other truth.

"You mean the girl that Sam brought in said someone set the fires intentionally...on purpose?" Bang had asked. The thought seemed ludicrous.

Graham remembered rubbing the palms of his sweaty hands along his jeans to dry them. "And there've been some strange reports lately. We don't really know what's going on. Radio reports are scattered." Graham had watched for his son's reaction. He was ready for any pending questions but there were none. Bang's expression became one of resolve. Perhaps it was only his eyes that grew stony cold. Graham wasn't sure. Bang only rose silently from the chair and went to bed.

That's what kept Graham up most of the night. It wasn't really the news of the coming danger of fire or the terrorists that set them, it was his son's reaction—or the lack of reaction. He wasn't sure what it meant, really. But when he heard the chirp of the radio keying in, he rose off his bed and wandered into the living room. He knew it was a wakeup call, courtesy of Dalton. It meant get ready...time to go. "Copy" was all Graham said, his voice coming out more groggily than he wanted it to.

"Bang, Tehya, time to get up and at them," he said loud enough to wake them. Then he started the coffee, which was actually made from roasted garbanzo beans since he had not taken the time to trade for the real stuff in ages. He liked the nutty flavor. Even though there was no caffeine in the brew, it was a morning ritual he still needed. Bang was the only one who complained; he still wanted the real thing. Sam slipped him the genuine stuff on occasion so Graham wasn't motivated to take up the caffeine addiction again.

"Five minutes, guys. Hurry up."

They grabbed their gear and were out the door before then, though. They'd trained well over the years. Human hygiene wasn't as obsessive as it was in times past. They stayed clean but only as time and work permitted. Showers were relegated to two to three times a week or when needed.

Bang said as they walked down the porch steps, "Aren't you going to lock the door?"

Graham stopped and looked back over his shoulder and shrugged. "No, we'll either return or we won't."

"But..." Tehya began.

And Graham didn't give her the chance to finish. "Get in, or we'll run late for our own evacuation."

As Graham loaded his own backpack into the back of the loaded truck, Bang tossed his gear in as well and then reached down and picked Sheriff up and helped into the back of the cab with Tehya, taking up half the back seat. Graham wasn't expecting that and Sheriff groaned a bit in protest as Bang lifted him. Just like an old man complaining when you tried to help him put on his jacket, Sheriff too looked a bit dejected.

"I'm just helping you, Sheriff. Stop complaining."

"He doesn't want you to help him," Tehya said with her brows furrowed. "He wants to do it himself."

Bang said nothing in return. He only caught Graham's eyes and settled into the passenger seat, avoiding any explanation.

Soon they were down the road, where smoke from the coming fires was thicker and the growing smell made all of them a little readier to evacuate. Entering Dalton's side, vehicles were packed and already in position to caravan out. The excitement further increased Graham's anxiety.

Graham pulled up behind the last vehicle and put the truck in park. He saw Clarisse struggling to handle two loaded baby carriers at once and said, "Tehya, go help Clarisse."

"I don't..." she began to say but Graham shot her a look that made her scramble out the door.

Bang was already headed in Sam and Addy's direction to help them before Graham could assign him a task. Graham stepped out of the truck and went to see what he could offer or where he could assist in getting things going. The prepper camp brought back memories, both good and bad. He remembered caring for Tala with her broken leg in quarantine, which only brought them closer together after that awful accident. He remembered escaping to the prepper camp and being just a few amongst the many living in tents to have safety in numbers as the terrorists gained ground.

Now the prepper camp was nearly half as populated. People moved on to other communities but this was their safe haven in the worst of times. Where Graham and Bang and a few lucky others were immune to the weaponized bird flu, these people lived on hope and prayer and they made it through after fighting for their lives in the most ruthless way ever. Many did not make it. Some could never forget it. And like Graham, many remembered because they lost someone then that they never wanted to forget.

"Graham, can you give me a hand?" Dalton said.

"Of course," he said as he watched an annoyed Tehya carrying a baby carrier loaded with a screaming infant to Dalton's truck.

He had to smile but didn't let his daughter see as he followed Dalton into the quarantine lab...it was now the 'hospital' but Graham would always think of it as its beginnings.

As Dalton led him into one of the rooms, Graham saw a young girl lying on a hospital bed, her hands and feet bandaged. Graham winced, seeing light yellow fluid seeping from the middle of one palm.

Dalton said, "This is Cheryl. Cheryl, this is Graham. He's one of our leaders here. Graham, can she ride with you and Tehya? I know it's a lot to ask," he added quickly. "We will have the babies with us in the other truck and Cheryl, as you can see, is recovering from her burns. She's not allowed to walk or drive any vehicles since she's under the influence of a strong painkiller."

Cheryl giggled at Dalton's joke as only a ten-year-old girl on medication would and began to nod off again.

She looked glassy-eyed and malnourished. She was all knees and elbows. Her dark hair had been cut at a short blunt just under her chin. Someone had taken good care of her at some point, but where was that person now? Almost resentful at Dalton for putting him in this position, Graham wanted to say no. He knew Dalton wanted him to take her on and that perhaps it would benefit Tehya in the end. He wasn't so sure. Tehya had her own mind; he wasn't sure if she'd accept a friend. But considering the predicament that Clarisse was in with the infants, he decided it was wise. She couldn't also take care of this girl in need as well while Dalton drove. The three infants were bad enough.

"Okay, she can sit in the back with Tehya and Sheriff," Graham said and widened his eyes at his friend, like, *I don't know about this.*

Dalton whispered, "If Tehya has a problem with this arrangement, tell her she's welcome to ride with us and *the babies.* Addy is coming along to help us too. Sam will have my boys."

Graham chuckled, "Yeah, that'll do it."

"Clarisse said she can't walk yet so we'll have to carry her. And she's a little loopy on the pain meds that Clarisse gave her. She'll probably sleep a lot. She keeps yelling for her mom in her sleep, poor thing."

"Okay, I'll report anything she might say. Might be good for Tehya to have someone her age to care for," Graham said as he lifted the sleeping girl into his arms. Dalton followed with several blankets and pillows, along with all the medical products the child needed.

"We'll stop as often as permitted and check on her. We think she needs a quieter space. Hard to sleep with one of three babies always crying in the next room."

"That's no problem but we'll have to move Sheriff over a bit. She weighs nearly nothing, Dalton. When's the last time she ate?"

"This morning. We have to take it slow, so she'll keep things down. We don't think she had anything in several days before Sam found her."

"Okay," he said and that's when he saw Bang carrying not one but two rifles. He looked at Dalton questioningly.

"All vehicles have a gunner. Bang is yours. He's been briefed."

Graham wanted to say, *Why didn't you ask me first?* But that was a question he would have asked in the old days. He couldn't help the initial reaction. He'd lived and resolved to a different way of thinking now. Bang was well trained. He was a great shot, in fact. He'd been briefed and would keep them safe.

"Who's on yours?"

"Pfft, I got the best of them. Addy's mine," Dalton laughed, and he was right.

Graham carried the girl out to his truck when a voice yelled, "Dalton!"

Graham turned to see what was so urgent and after Dalton got the message, he yelled to everyone else, "Let's go! Leave the rest behind; everyone in your vehicles, now."

People scrambled then. Every vehicle would soon fill with its assigned members and then they would leave immediately. No one asked why they were leaving five minutes earlier than originally planned; they did what they were told. Graham opened the back seat door and Sheriff looked up startled from his place on the seat. Sliding the girl into the middle, Graham crowded Sheriff and buckled her inside.

Sheriff barked lightly and whined a little suddenly as Graham began to help Tehya inside too.

"What's his problem?" Tehya said.

The girl named Cheryl was barely conscious and leaned over the dog's side.

Sheriff continued to sniff the girl and look to Graham as if he had a question.

"I...I don't know. He's never acted that way before," Graham said, and worried that his old friend was declining faster than he thought.

"Maybe he just doesn't like being crowded," Tehya said. "Does she have to ride with us? I don't like being crowded either," Tehya said as she scrambled into the other side, eyeing the sleeping girl.

Graham just gave his daughter a push into her seat, while Bang climbed in the passenger side, window down and rifle at the ready.

"Why does she have to ride with us anyway?" Tehya dared another protest and before Graham could correct his daughter, Bang said, "Quiet, Tehya," sharp enough to reprimand his little sister into silence, which didn't stop her from glaring at the back of her brother's head.

With the engine started and ready to go, Graham watched as Bang looked ahead of them to Dalton's truck. He knew his son and he knew he was checking on Addy. Graham watched as Addy gave Bang a thumbs-up and when they started rolling out of camp, Bang did the same back to his friend.

# 15

# RICK

"We're putting the roadblock up right before Huetter's Rest area. There's more staging area and it's uphill, easier to see things coming in from the west," said McCann over the radio.

"Good planning. You've certainly learned defensive tactics. Head back when you have the assigned crew there. Your wife's getting antsy," Rick said. When he looked over at her she was, of course, glaring at him. Teasing the younger generation was his daily entertainment; he lived for the zingers as often as possible. And keeping them in a lighter mood when they could all be pulling their hair out helped as well.

"You and your sister have the children ready for departure if needed?" Rick asked Macy, though he knew he was in for an earful.

"Marcy has the children prepped if needed. The ferry boat is set for Harrison, on the far end of the lake. I am staying here. You forget that I'm needed for radio communication in your absence."

He stood over her then and said in a firm voice. "You *will* get on that ferry, when I ask you to, Macy. You understand? Or I will sedate you and your unborn child, which might cause harm, but if I have to, I will. Capisce?"

"You wouldn't," she said, leaning back in her chair suddenly.

"I will...try me. I've done it before, don't you remember? I'll do it again. To protect that infant from your bullheadedness, I will."

A pinkish hue rose in her cheeks but she nodded. All kidding aside, Rick was prepared to do *anything* it took to keep everyone he was in charge of safe. No matter what. They'd lost too many lives overall.

Just then a radio call came in and Rick answered. "Left five minutes ago. Got word the fire was jumping the Skagit River to the west with an easterly wind. Headed this way, over."

The voice belonged to Dalton. And suddenly the old and more formal clipped radio lingo was in effect. They'd become casual with communications over time without cellphones, but in a moment of danger, the more formal short tone was on again.

"Copy," Rick said, just like in old times. "Stay frosty. Out."

Macy heard the call. Her solemn gaze and straight mouth told him she was worried.

"What about Liberty Lake, Bonner's Ferry, and the other smaller communities around here?" Macy asked him suddenly.

"What about them?"

"Well, there are still a few people living out there. Smaller communities but they're there. Even Lucy went back to Liberty Lake once she got married last year. She's one of us. We can't leave her out there if the fires get that bad...or whatever." No one wanted to voice what they feared.

Rick shook his head. Their protocol was that anyone outside of the boundary was on their own. That was their choice. "Contact leaders and tell them to get over here before sundown or they're locked out. We had this protocol set in place years ago. It's just been in the last three that we've let things get too relaxed. Everyone's forgotten there are major dangers, like fires, or people on the planet that still have an axe to grind. Okay, maybe that wasn't the best analogy right now."

"No, not really appropriate...considering," Macy said, glaring at him.

"Be that as it may, we save who we can, Graham's camp being the satellite exception; they're family...and Lucy. Right now, the fire is the imminent threat for Graham's camp. We have to keep Graham's camp one step in front of the fire the whole way here."

"That's not as easy as it used to be when you could track us."

"I know, now we're back to old school. Radio calls and paper maps. At this rate, we might end up devolving even further. Radio will never fail us though, that's for sure."

"Only if you have access to a radio and an antenna and relay if needed," Macy countered.

"Well, yeah...and a few other factors. Like someone who knows how to operate one on the other end."

He smiled at Macy as she tilted her head to one side quickly. They were realistic now. That was his takeaway from the conversation. Life was not guaranteed. People died of silly things now. Preventable things. Exhaustion was one of them. Man was not made like he used to be; it would take generations of hard physical labor to bring that back.

"When does McCann get back?" Macy asked, interrupting his thoughts.

"Maybe an hour or more. I'm not his keeper, you are."

"You are when he's under your orders," Macy said.

Having no snarky come back for that one, he ignored her and tracked Graham's camp on the paper map in front of him while Macy made the radio calls to the nearby communities to come into the fold, like a shepherd calling in the flock.

# 16

## GRAHAM

"What did she say?" Graham asked as he drove.

"She keeps mumbling something," Tehya said, shaking her head. "I don't understand her."

Looking at the girl lying in the back seat next to his daughter, Graham saw that she was jerking and terrified of something in a dream. Even Sheriff seemed to be trying to comfort the girl. He continued to sniff her and laid his muzzle along her side. Then she suddenly screamed, "Mom!" and her eyes opened wide.

"Dad!" Tehya said, startled. Even Sheriff jerked up from the loud noise and whined occasionally as he lay next to the girl.

"Keep her quiet," Bang told his sister, while he kept his attention on the radio monitor and kept vigilant to what was going on outside the vehicle.

Tehya's eyebrows furrowed and she glared at her brother again.

Graham said, "Try to keep her calm. Give her a drink. Talk to her, Tehya."

He watched his daughter as she engaged the girl, looking terrified at her surroundings, and tried to comfort her as Sheriff, too, settled down.

"Where's your mom?" Tehya asked her.

"She's...she's like my mom. She's not really my mom," Cheryl said.

"Where is she now?" Tehya asked while she gave Cheryl the water bottle to hold between her bandaged hands.

Cheryl pulled the bottle up to her lips and drank deeply. Water trickled out of the side of her mouth in a little stream.

Tehya took the bottle from her and screwed the cap back on while Cheryl answered. "I don't know. She helped me get away from the tents. We were near the big city then. It was on fire. The fire came fast. It's all on fire now. They didn't know." Tears now streamed down Cheryl's face. It was too much too soon. Whatever the girl had been through, it was too traumatic an event for her to recall.

Graham smiled at his daughter, looking to him for help in the rearview mirror.

"It's okay, Cheryl. We'll try to find your mom and help her too," Graham watched as his daughter put an arm around the upset child to comfort her. Empathy was something new to Tehya, and Graham was relieved his daughter was gifted with the concept just then.

"Dad," Bang said suddenly.

"What?"

"Dalton says we're to stop soon."

"Gotcha. Maybe we can give Cheryl some more pain meds then."

Teyha held the girl in the back seat and nodded her head solemnly.

Then Graham saw brake lights and slowed to a stop. Had Bang not warned him of the scheduled stop, Graham still would have known that something was up. Hand signals had taken over with the scouts on convoys, a silent but effective way of communicating with the vehicle behind you.

"Why are we stopping?" Tehya asked.

"Probably low on fuel," Graham said after checking his gauge. Then the gas cans came out from the drivers ahead of them. He too got out, even though he had a larger tank than the pickup in front of him, and lifted the gas can from the back of the vehicle to top off his tank.

In the early days, after the collapse, they'd rerefined the fuel from stranded vehicles by siphoning off tanks. Fuel begins to go bad after a month. After six months, a grit forms in the tank hard enough to mark up the inside, and forget about the fuel lines and fittings. Running that stuff through your engine is a death knell. So to use the fuel, it must be rerefined.

Any vehicle newer than 1989 was useless to them for this purpose because rerefined fuel would basically eat through the plastic seals and fittings. Instead, the older model vehicles with actual carburetors rather than electronic fuel injection were the only ones that could handle the raw fuel, even with ethanol mixed in. Otherwise the cruder fuel would burn the daylights right out of the sensors, which defeated the purpose if you wanted to get somewhere.

Even so, the engines sputtered and smoked like mad. This is where Sam came in. On his scavenging trips, among his many jobs were siphoning off the tanks of stranded vehicles, stealing parts from them if they were useful and marking them with a big X, indicating that they were harvested already. Then, when he returned, he poured the fuel into a still built far from camp which was basically a large drum with a fire lit underneath it. Quite a bit more complicated than that, but that's the basic model. Someone sat there and monitored the process from behind a cinderblock wall just in case there was an explosion.

Another method for finding and using gasoline was from gas pipelines. Sam and a few others had heard of a guy in Montana who used to harvest fuel directly from the pipeline traps. This was harsh stuff but again it would run in the older model engines...after complaining.

But as time went on, scavenging for gasoline was a thing of the past. Anything found in a stranded vehicle wasn't even worth harvesting eight years from the collapse, since the liquid gas had long turned to a solid state. It was time to either go strictly horse and buggy again or refine fuel the old-fashioned way, and Sam devised yet another still application to refine fuel from basic crude oil, like they did in the old, old days. From crude oil, they could make diesel and gasoline, and oil wells are pressured without the need for artificial lift to get the crude out.

Long story short, Sam was now an oilman as well as a scavenger and finder of lost children, apparently. Graham laughed at Sam's evolution from mountain man to oil man over the years as he topped off his tank and waved away the harsh fumes.

"Dad!" Bang yelled.

When he looked up, he saw Clarisse running their way.

# 17

# RICK

"Rick?" Dalton said over the radio.

"Yeah?" Rick said after a few seconds.

"We're stopped on Highway 20 still to refuel right outside of the Gorge Overlook Trail, and we've found something."

"What? Another child? Not another baby?"

"No," he chuckled, "a blond woman around thirty this time. She came running at us from up the hill. I nearly shot her. I swear, I'm not as steady as I once was."

Rick nodded and looked up at Macy. "None of us are, my friend. Maybe she's a match to one of those kids that you have there."

"We'll see. She's terrified. Says men are setting fires near Bellingham now. To the south we can see there's a big fire near Lake Chelan. Many of the overgrown fruit groves look demolished. They were dry tinder anyway without being watered regularly. We'll have to keep north and skirt the border again. We'll stay on 20 as long as possible."

"There's fire south of Winthrop and Twisp. I'm worried about that area. That's where I had the kids turn around."

"We don't have a lot of choices here, Rick. We'll keep heading east on 20 and strike Highway 97 north at Okanogan and see from there.

I'll keep you posted. Wait, Clarisse is yelling at me. Hold on," Dalton said.

Rick raised his eyebrow at Macy, who looked worried.

"Hey," Dalton came back a second later, "seems the woman is looking for the girl named Cheryl. We actually did find a match, it seems."

"That's great news!" Rick said.

"She's the girl's mom, I think. I'll let you know more when we get closer."

"Be careful through that winding narrow road, Dalton. Watch out for traps."

"Copy. Don't worry, we will. Not our first rodeo, nor our last, I predict. Out."

# 18

# GRAHAM

"What's going on?" Graham asked Clarisse, who was out of breath.

"We found a woman up ahead. She warned us of the fires to the south. She said she's looking for a girl." Clarisse pointed to inside the truck. "I think she's looking for Cheryl."

"Are you sure? She's over ten miles east of where she was found. Cheryl's really out of it. I don't know that we should traumatize her right now. She's having nightmares." Inwardly Graham chastised himself for already forming a bond with the injured child he so carefully put into the back of his truck. To him that meant she was his to protect. Why did he always connect to the strays? *That's it, I'm staying away from the babies.*

"We haven't told her about the girl yet. We'll see what she knows for now. She's injured and dehydrated. She has burns on her forearms as well. She says the fires are being set on purpose by men that kidnapped them near Mount Rainer."

"What kind of men?" Inside, his stomach felt as if it was dissolving as he quickly glanced to his kids inside the truck.

Clarisse shook her head. "I don't know yet. We'll keep questioning her. She said they barely spoke English. I'm afraid we are dealing with our old enemy."

"How the hell is that possible, Clarisse?"

She shook her head. "It's a war of science at this point. It's possible there were many immune, just like you were, and they reformed with the same sick religion of hate they hold for us. Unfortunately, there is nothing I can do to eradicate the hate in men. I can only kill the men with the hate," she said in a soft voice with her eyebrows raised.

He knew the consequences of what she did the last time still weighed heavily on her soul. And yet it didn't bother Graham one bit. And that's why he questioned his own resolve now. He'd do it all over again to save them, with the exception of somehow saving Tala as well. He held no remorse for the deaths of those terrorists and now he was changed in a way he never thought he could be in his youth. In a way, it was a horrible resolution.

Putting the gas can back in its secure place, he hugged Clarisse and whispered, "We will do whatever it takes, again and again and again. As long as it takes, Clarisse. I'm surprised we haven't had another wave in eight years. We've had pockets here and there but not another wave of terrorists coming from their homeland. Let's show them what we've got, again. You're prepared, right?"

Her eyes were watery when she pulled away. She pushed her glasses up and wiped the moisture underneath. Nodding her head, she said, "I think so. But we'll have to test again, and you know what that means."

Nodding, he said, "*Whatever* it takes."

Clarisse began to walk away but Graham called her back "Hey Clarisse, what's her name?"

"The woman we just found?"

"Yeah."

"She said her name is Paige."

# AFTERWORD

I hope you enjoyed *The Bitter Earth, Book 5 in the Graham's Resolution series*. Book 6 in this series is currently in the works as well as several other projects. As a side note, Enzo is named after a Spokane, WA, police dog. You can see Enzo and his friends' news on Friend's of Spokane County K9s.

To be among the first to learn about new releases, announcements, and special projects, please follow this link. (ebook only for print follow the link below to my website.) You can also drop me a note from that location. You can also order signed paperback copies on this link.

\*\*\*Above all, **please leave a review** for *The Bitter Earth* on Amazon. Even a quick word about your experience can be helpful to prospective readers.

While you're waiting for the next book in the *Graham's Resolution* series, you can enjoy the bestselling series of *Surrender the Sun* , the first few chapters of the first novel follow toward the end.

Thank you,
AR Shaw

# ABOUT THE AUTHOR

*What the world dreads most has happened*, is the tagline of A. R. Shaw's work and that statement give you an idea of where her stories often lead, into the abyss of destruction and mayhem with humanity thrown in as a complication. She writes realistic scenarios which are often the worries in the dark of night. So far, she's sold over 51 thousand books and only just begun. A. R. Shaw resides somewhere in the Pacific Northwest.

*For more information*
AuthorARShaw.com
Annette@AuthorARShaw.com

[f]

Sample of Surrender the Sun, Book 1

Chapter 1
October 31, 2030
Coeur d'Alene, Idaho

Lying on her blanket-strewn queen-sized bed, the one she'd once shared with Roger, Maeve dreamed. He was there again...with her, laughing as she complained about him leaving his coffee cups everywhere in the garage growing islands of fluffy green mold. "It wouldn't kill you to put them in the dishwasher yourself, you know."

Levering open the dishwasher door, she made a show of turning the dirty mug upside down and placing it on the top rack. "See, it's that easy. Even easy enough for *you* to do." He grabbed her around the waist and tickled her until she squealed.

"Easy, huh?" But the tone of his voice meant something entirely different than the ease of washing moldy mugs.

But as she glanced down, pasty blood covered his camo trousers, causing them to turn a shade of puce as the red mingled with the brown. She begged him to release her and knew the deceit of the scene then.

As he quickly lifted her up into his embrace, she stole one last look into his eyes before the dream faded and he was snatched from her again. Before he left her, she reached up and pressed her hands against his rough cheeks, engulfing him so that she would remember him this time, the feel of his pressed lips to hers. She held the illusion even as his form began to dissipate no matter how hard she willed to hang on to him. "I love you. Don't leave me."

Her hand moved over the soft, rumpled sheets then, in the space he should have been but would never be again. Burying her face into the covers, she sobbed as dawn brought yet another day with the realization she'd lost him forever.

"Mom?"

Maeve wiped away the tears before she turned to her six-year-old son standing in the doorway. "Good morning, Ben. I'll be up in just a second, buddy."

"You were dreaming again. I heard you."

Like many mornings before, she needed to divert the conversation, or they'd both end up in turmoil with past memories and ghosts haunting them throughout the day. "Hey," she said, "you have a Halloween party today, right?"

"Uh huh," he said as he padded barefoot to her bedside. She pulled him closer. Ben's little boy smell still made her ache. His features were so like Roger's, set in miniature. His dark hair and brown eyes were the color of milk chocolate. She adored that Ben resembled his father more than herself. At least she had a permanent part of her dead husband after all.

She brushed her son's overgrown bangs out of his eyes then hugged him tighter. She knew he sensed her sadness. Fending off her emotions, she needed to pull strength from somewhere else deep inside for the both of them today. This was the wrong way to start the day; she knew that by repetition.

Drawing a smile to her lips, she kissed him. "Go get your cowboy costume on and I'll get in the shower. Scoot."

"OK, can I have cereal for breakfast this morning?"

"That would be far too much sugar with class treats later today. How about some oatmeal instead?"

He nodded and then sprinted down the carpeted hallway to his bedroom as she yelled, "Walk please."

Resigned to the fact that she now had to start the day, Maeve sat up and pulled her legs over the side of the bed. Running her hands through her long red hair, she tried to pull her wild mane behind her. In doing so, she glanced at the picture on her bedside table. The image with her and Roger and the infant Ben. The proud parents that somehow made this miracle stared back out at her with perfectly drawn happiness in their expressions; not a hint of tragedy marred their faces.

The Maeve today barely recognized those people. How the pain of losing Roger hurt as if his death had happened just the day before! She resented the picture now. How could they've been so happy? Didn't they know the life they led couldn't last for very long? People died in war. Fathers, mothers, brothers, sisters, and her husband along with them. Why did they think they were immune to death? The image brought her no more joy. It only brought her jealousy now. She kept the photo there on her night-stand out of tradition, hoping that someday she'd feel something more beyond bitter resentment for having him ripped from her and her son.

*Not like this. Not today.*

Maeve ran her fingers through her hair again and shook them, causing her hair to wave around wildly. *Ugh, get going,* she said to herself to shed the malaise trying to possess her today. She whipped the covers to the side and moved herself to the edge of the bed. Without the warmth of the covers, she realized she could see her breath out before her in her own room. *No wonder Ben ran to his room. It's freezing in here.* She hurried to the adjoining bathroom. Starting the shower, more to warm the space than herself, Maeve removed her nightshirt and brushed her teeth as they chattered from the invading freezing temperatures.

As the room began to fog with warm steam, she stepped into the water, still clutching the toothbrush between her teeth. She would take any compromise to warm herself, and if that meant brushing in the shower, so be it.

A haze wafted up around her as she turned in the warm cascading spray and then finished the task. Once thoroughly warmed and cleaned, she dressed for the day, reluctant to leave the soothing heat of the small bathroom. Then she descended the stairs of the A-frame house and landed on the cold wood floor on the main level.

Switching on her iPad that she kept in the kitchen, she set the station to the local live news stream out of Spokane while she turned on the Keurig and began Ben's oatmeal.

"It's cold in here, Mom. I can even see my breath," Ben said as he entered the room dressed in his cowboy getup, minus the holster and six-shooters that the school frowned upon. Joining her in the kitchen, he climbed up on the barstool while watching his mom carry on with their morning routine.

"I noticed. Maybe the furnace is out," she said, and while the Keurig emitted a welcome scent, she stepped over into the hallway near the garage and checked the regulator on the wall. "I don't know. It says sixty-seven. I can hear the furnace running. I'll push it up a little anyway. I'll have to call someone to come out and check it today."

"Look at the news, Mom," Ben said. "There's a snowstorm."

She followed his small finger pointing to the screen. The weatherman was expressing concern over the new weather disturbance coming their way. "Great, and at the end of October, too," Maeve said. She finished making her coffee while she watched the news report with her son on the iPad screen.

*"KREX News reporting. Bob Madeira here. Folks, bundle up. The lowest recorded temperature in the Spokane region is seven degrees recorded back in 2002. I hate to break it to you, but it's five degrees out there right now. I'm sure there's a lot of broken pipes in the region, and area plumbers will be out in full force today. Especially for those who haven't blown out their sprinklers yet, like me...*

*"Residents in Coeur d'Alene are enjoying three-degree weather this morning. In fact, let's check the forecast for this week—woo wee, it's going to be a shiver-fest. The highs are well below freezing the rest of this week and into the next. Most schools have either closed for the day, or there's a two-hour late start. Check your local school. It's a deep freeze, folks, with no end in sight..."*

"Fantastic!" Maeve said with a chill.

"Is it going to snow?" Ben asked with excitement. His eyes sprung wide.

"Oh...I hope not. I never thought that stuff would melt off last year. Eat your oatmeal," Maeve said and plunked his bowl down in front of him. "I'm going to start the truck and get the engine warmed up before we go."

She set her hot coffee cup down reluctantly. Maeve slid into her boots and pulled her black puffy coat on, then opened the door to the garage and felt the meaning of freezing cold hitting her face. "Three degrees, my arse...Ugh, oh." She fumbled with her zipper as her fingers became numbed. "Gosh darn it, friggin' cold out here," she grumbled on her way to the driver's side of her cream-and-black SUV, a Toyota FJ Cruiser.

Once behind the wheel, she hit the garage door opener and then put the keys in the ignition. Then the garage door made a sound unlike its usual racket. "What the heck?" she said, looking in the rearview mirror. The door remained in place.

She pressed the door opener again, and this time, it lifted maybe two inches before giving up and closing once again. "Damn thing's frozen, man..."

Maeve stepped out of the FJ. "What would Roger do?" She'd uttered this phrase countless times since his death, and it had helped her figure out how to handle many tasks in the past, though now she knew it was a reliance she needed to let go of.

She scanned his workbench, remembering him squirting something from a blue spray bottle that he kept inside the door during the coldest months of winter.

"Where is that thing?"

She rifled through a few boxes of random automotive bottles and then found the one she was looking for. Maeve unscrewed the lid and smelled the contents. "Vinegar?" After replacing the top, she shook the contents. Though she knew the concoction was a year old, she hoped the solution would still work.

She began spraying the door's seal, hoping to melt whatever was frozen. Again she tried the door after waiting a few seconds, and though the door did open, it opened a bit slower, like a cranky old man rising from his bed with enough complaints and resentment to color the rest of his day with a bad attitude.

Maeve stood there looking at the frozen landscape outside her home in amazement. She could swear the month was January instead of October: everything was covered in a determined layer of frost and appeared brittle before its time. The sugar maple in her front yard had yet to lose all of its bronzed leaves—each leaf perfectly caught in a colorful stagnation now encapsulated in white crystals. Mounds of leaves were scattered everywhere over the graveled driveway and covered with a thick layer of icy frost. The long road leading to their private twenty acres within the Coeur d'Alene National Forest was beset with wild critter trails, their footsteps marking their paths from an early emergence of the day regardless of the human interlopers.

She blew out an icy breath. "Wonderful…" Though she didn't think the conditions were really any kind of *wonderful.* She meant the statement as sarcasm—the beauty of the frozen scene was undeniably a beautiful winter scene, just far too early in autumn.

She turned on her heel and started the FJ; this time though, it took two tries to get the cold engine to comply with her request. She remembered Roger telling her once that cold weather was as hard on engines as it was on people. She doubted him then, though now it seemed his statement was redeemed.

"Ben, get your big coat on and gloves and your hat," she said as she entered the now-warmed house once again.

"Do I have to? No one else will be wearing theirs," Ben complained.

"No, you don't, but take one step out there without your warmest gear on and you'll lose your nose to frostbite. You don't really need those fingers either, do you?" She shook her head in mock agreement.

"Mom!" Ben rolled his eyes.

"Seriously, you heard the weatherman. Bundle up, buddy."

"OK," Ben said as he climbed off the stool, taking big steps with slumped shoulders up the stairs. He finished his morning routine with the reluctant addition of winter gear while Maeve finished her now lukewarm coffee, cleaned out Ben's breakfast bowl, and listened to the news while she packed their lunches and grabbed her gear for the day.

As Maeve pulled out of the long driveway and drove away from the house, she was thankful for the choppy gravel drive. She would have slid on the sloped icy frost halfway down the path without the benefit of the grit. However, once she pulled off of Scenic Bay Drive onto the nicely paved Beauty Bay Drive, she began sliding to the other side of the road. The slick street made it nearly impossible to gain traction even after she put the FJ into four-wheel drive.

"Well, that wasn't the way I'd planned it."

"You're a bad driver," Ben announced with confidence from the back seat.

She checked her son in the rearview mirror, arched her eyebrow, and asked, "Whoever told you that I was a *bad* driver?"

"That's what Grandpa Jack says."

Maeve let out a frustrated breath. "I am *not* a bad driver. Grandpa Jack tells that story of when I was *learning* to drive. I haven't run into a police officer since I was a teenager." She began to drive down their sparsely inhabited road as she left. "I'm going to have to have a talk with Grandpa Jack next time we go to Maine. What are you laughing about back there?"

Ben giggled again. "You," he said, pointing. "Ran into a *policeman!*"

"Agh! Some things you never live down. I swear even your..."

She swallowed hard. She'd done it again. She'd forgotten...As impossible as it was to forget her husband's death, it happened from time to time, even now. "Even your dad used to give me a hard time about that one." She ended her statement with a smile and then glanced in the rearview mirror to see how Ben had taken the mention of his father again.

She found him with a half-smile staring out the window. It wasn't *so* bad now. A month ago she couldn't even mention Roger's name without Ben and herself resorting to tears still or at least a painful knot in their throats. Now, it was just the painful knot and a clenched stomach. *Time heals all wounds? That's a trick I'd like to see*, she thought, still glancing at her boy's reflection as he appeared to brace for impact.

"Mom!" Ben shouted with his arm outstretched. With a sickening crunch, a blurry rust-brown beast flitted to the side of the road. Careening recklessly, the SUV skidded out of control, finally coming to a stop on the icy, narrow, winding two-lane street.

Her heart pounding like a racing piston, Maeve turned to her son. "Ben! Are you all right?" Her hands shook like leaves. "Ben?"

"Yes, Mom, I'm fine. You hit him, I think?"

"Was it a deer? A moose? I didn't even see what it was." She scanned the windows to catch a glimpse with hopes she hadn't killed the unknown creature.

"You hit a *man*, Mom! It was a man on a horse. It was the hermit guy, I bet."

"Oh my goodness!"

"You hit him, Mom!"

"Oh jeez," she said. There were tracks in the icy frost on the road leading off the side and into the forest, but she didn't see anyone, man or beast, out there anywhere.

Sitting sideways in the middle of the road, she restarted the SUV and then pulled the truck over to the side of the road with her emergency flashing lights on. "Stay right here, Ben," she said as she released her seatbelt that now clenched across her lap like a vise. This stretch of Beauty Bay Road traversing through the thick forest was always her favorite part. She could breathe deeply here in its seclusion and felt peace unlike anywhere else in the world. It wasn't until five more miles up the two-lane road that her breath became more shallow and tense as the small town of Coeur d'Alene came into view.

Roger often told her the thickly forested area was home to several ex-military men who just couldn't take society anymore after the trauma of war and used the forest as a sanctuary of sorts. They lived off the land there, and now Maeve was afraid she'd just killed or maimed one of them, the one they called the Hermit.

"Hello?" she shouted after she quickly shut the door to keep the warmth inside of the truck for Ben. She cupped her hands around her mouth and yelled, "I didn't mean to hurt you. Are you all right?" She waited for a response as she followed the tracks in the frost leading from the road into the evergreen forest. They became harder to detect the farther she went, as the canopy of the woods held back the frost and the evidence of footprints. Once, two feet in the dense brush, she looked back at Ben looking through the truck window after her. Her breath puffed out in little clouds in front of her face.

Her nose was already numb, and her cheeks felt frozen solid. She crossed her arms and suddenly had the feeling someone was watching her, and though she was cold, there was something more making her shiver.

"I'm sorry I hit you. Please let me help," she yelled again, breaking the solitude of the forest. That's when she finally saw him and had the feeling it was only because he'd *let* her see him. A man hidden in plain sight appeared before her. Wearing military camo much like Roger's, he blended in well with the evergreen surroundings.

His raspy voice startled her. It was as if he hadn't used it in quite some time. "Don't yell. You should watch where you're going. Especially with a kid in the car," he said, motioning toward the SUV.

Her mouth agape, she finally said, "I...I'm sorry. Did I hurt you or your horse?"

"You almost did. He's fine. I think you murdered a few fallen branches on the road though. Go on. Just watch where you're going," he said gruffly, but his eyes were soft and unyielding as he held her attention.

"Can I bring you anything?" she said, assuming he was the hermit Ben mentioned.

"I have everything I need."

She took the hint that he wanted her to leave. "OK. OK then. I'm Maeve Tildon," she said and held out her hand for him to shake.

He stared at the offering.

Her hand hanging in midair for longer than a comfortable time, she let it drop. "If you find out later that you, or your horse, are hurt... well, I live down Scenic Bay Road. There's a sign on the mailbox that says Tildon. You can't miss us. Just let me know. I'll pay for any medical expenses or vet bills," she said and turned her head toward her SUV, then suddenly turned back again. "I'm just *very* sorry." As if she really wanted him to know she truly was.

He nodded at her and diverted his vision to the side.

She figured that was the end of their short conversation, and she turned to leave again.

"Hey, you're Maeve? Roger's Maeve?"

She turned. "Yeah. I mean, I...Roger...he died. Over...there."

The man stood there a moment, silent, maneuvering the news around in his head as if a puzzle piece he'd tried to fit into place had found home. She knew the feeling.

"I hadn't heard. I'm sorry. When?"

Caught off guard, she said, "Almost a year now. Did you know him?"

He took a step back. "Yeah. I knew Roger."

She responded the way she always did. With sad eyes, she smiled slightly because there was no way to respond appropriately to having someone ripped from you. If there was, she hadn't figured it out yet. She turned, and when she did, she did it into herself. Set back a mile in grief in an instant, again.

She walked back to the opening from the forest to her truck holding her son. Then she turned, and this time when she looked back, the man was gone. Vanished into the woods.

She never did see the horse she'd nearly hit.

Shaking her head as if his image had been a dream, she made her way back to the SUV and climbed inside, noticing it was nearly as cold inside now as it was outside. Ben was shivering in his car seat.

"Did you find the Hermit?"

"I found a *man*. It's not nice to call someone a hermit, Ben."

She started the truck.

"What's his name then? That's what they call him at school. He has a horse. Was the horse hurt?"

"Far too many questions all at once, son. He didn't mention his name, and it looks like they're both fine, thank goodness." She lowered the emergency brake handle and restarted the engine.

"Let's go. You're going to be late for school this morning."

# C hapter 2

MAEVE OPENED the bookshop door with the force of her body and leaned hard against the glass door pane. Once inside, she was so cold that her breath was as apparent inside as out. "Don't they have the furnace on yet?" she said with no one to hear since her employees were not scheduled to arrive until later in the afternoon when business typically picked up.

She shook off her gloves and squeezed her fingers open and shut, trying to get them to work like normal.

She'd barely made it into town after dropping Ben off at Fernan Elementary School. Everyone remarked how terribly cold it was so early in October. Admonishments that the school should have called a two-hour-late session were whispered none too quietly down the hallways.

"Don't stand outside for me," she'd told her son. "Wait inside until you see me in the turnaround. OK, Ben?" She didn't want him to freeze outside after school, and sometimes the teacher's aides couldn't be trusted to take the right care in severe weather.

"Yes, Mom," he'd said, but she still doubted his words; he would be given to peer pressure and little boy attitudes by the end of the day.

Still, she stifled her motherly fears knowing he'd be fine, and while she doubted there would be much traffic today with the weather, she got the bookstore ready anyway. Perhaps a few patrons would come out just to get warm in her bookstore after watching the latest hit at the movie theater less than a block away.

Maeve opened the bookstore when Roger was deployed with some inheritance money she gained after her mother had passed away. She had hoped the work would be enough to divert her from her husband's absence. The new Stoneriver complex proved to be a great asset to Coeur d'Alene with its new theater and shops. Several restaurants occupied the once-vacant stores, and with the almost occupied condos above, they were certainly out of the financial woes that were present when the complex started back in the early 2000s.

She'd only just started making headway in the ledger books when she was notified of Roger's untimely death. Now, she hoped the shop's income would be enough to support her and Ben the rest of the way. Roger's retirement she didn't touch. Those funds went into an account exclusively for Ben to someday use as his college trust as he saw fit. At least there was that. She didn't have to worry about where the money for college would come from.

The few employees Maeve kept did inventory in the evenings and worked part-time on the weekends while the others filled in. Maeve kept herself for Ben most weekends and worked days until he was out of school. That way, he would have some semblance of a normal life. That was how she saw it in her mind anyway. A normal life for a little boy without a father. One she could never replace anyway.

After turning on the cash register computer system, Maeve checked the back door and looked for any packages left for her. She'd been expecting a shipment from Ingram Content any day, and though today would mark the shipment one day late, she wasn't worried. The ice on the roads was holding everything back; she'd already received a shipping delay notice in her e-mail.

A familiar jingle caught her attention. She returned to the front of the store, only to find Elizabeth, the lady that ran the sports store next door, standing inside.

"Maeve."

"Yes, I'm here," she said as she rounded the many shelves containing the books she loved.

"Did you hear?"

"Hear what?"

"The water pipes in my unit froze and burst. There's no water."

"No, I didn't hear. Are they coming to fix it?"

"No, not yet. All the condos above are also out of water. Isn't this something? Three degrees at the end of October? At this rate, we'll be in a deep freeze by Christmas."

"Oh gosh, don't even say that."

"Well, it's true. Didn't you hear about the preordained Ice Age? Many scientists have predicted this for a long time. It's all over the news. I remember my mother talking about it when I was a teenager. She said the same thing happened back in 1645 and the Thames in southern England froze over. They ice-skated on the river. There are old paintings about it. 'It's happened before. It'll happen again,'" she said. "Like an abusive husband." Elizabeth laughed.

"Are you going to close up shop then?" Maeve asked, thinking closing up might be a good idea for her, too.

"I have to stick around and wait for the plumber to show up. *If* he shows up. But you could go home. I doubt anyone'll venture out today anyway. The streets are terribly slick, and they've closed the theater."

"School's open, though."

"Ben went in then, did he? I heard they were going to let out early."

"Well, if that's the case, I should just call Angelina and Justin and have them stay home. I'll just pick up Ben and go home and watch movies all day. Maybe make some soup and popcorn."

"That's a splendid idea. You deserve to take some time off, Maeve."

Again Maeve half smiled and backed away. Her widowhood always came up, no matter how subtle the conversation. She backed a little more and said, "Well, call me if anything happens, then. I'll just close up the store and head back and pick up Ben on the way." Maeve flipped off the cash register and then asked, "Did they say what the high today would be?"

Her friend stepped back inside the store quickly. "I heard *this* is it. Three degrees. That's why it's such a big deal. I bet I don't get any trick-or-treaters tonight with this cold weather."

"Ugh, that's right. Halloween. I might take Ben by your place, but the roads are so slick, and if this keeps up by dark it'll be more like zero degrees. Too cold to take little ones out."

"I agree, and not safe to drive on the frozen streets. Do you have anyone nearby to walk him to?"

Maeve shook her head, "No, we're out in Beauty Bay. Might as well be the boonies. We like it that way, usually."

"You could bring him to our house. Sam's home—I'll call him to have something ready; it's on your way home anyway. Then head back. I bet Halloween will be canceled for a lot of children this year. Too bad, but it's safer that way, certainly not worth frostbite."

"Thank you. That's very sweet of you, but like you said, we'll just go straight home." Maeve could always count on her friend for quick parenting advice. "I'll lock up and go get him now."

A FEW MINUTES LATER, Maeve pulled up into the school parking lot. As she walked toward the green-painted school bell of Fernan Elementary School, she wasn't surprised to see they'd put down salt on the icy parking lot again to keep the parents from colliding into one another. She also wasn't surprised to see that several parents also had the practical idea of picking their kids up early on this treacherous weather day. The parking lot was full to overflowing. Why they didn't cancel classes in the first place confounded her.

"Hi, Maeve. Ben is in the cafeteria with the rest of the class," his teacher said as she passed by. "Did you get the text alert on your phone? Some parents are saying they didn't receive theirs."

"No, I just thought I'd close up my shop and come by early to get him because of the weather."

"That was smart of you. The furnace isn't working here, and we can't hold class in the frigid classrooms, so we alerted the call-in system, which apparently isn't working either."

"Gosh, I hope you get home early, too. It's supposed to get even colder in a few hours."

"I know. I'm worried. We live out toward the Palouse hills, and my kids have to walk quite a ways to our farm from the bus stop, and it's way too cold for exposed noses. I have to get my entire class home before I can leave and try to catch them before they start the walk home."

"I'm sorry. That's the opposite end of the lake for me, or I'd offer to help. Well, I'll get Ben out of here. I hope you get to leave earlier," Maeve said on her way to the cafeteria. She jogged a little down the hall and felt guilty, but something was telling her to hurry home. In the pit of her stomach, a funny feeling advised her to get Ben and get home *now*. Maeve rounded the corner of the cafeteria when she heard the principal, Mrs. Campbell, announce to all the children:

"Boys and girls, sometimes we have weather emergencies that might affect our plans. So I would like for each of you to please be responsible for yourselves and your younger siblings. It's simply not safe for trick-or-treating tonight, and so we are thankful that you've each been able to spend your holiday indoors with us today. When you go home, I want you all to stay safely inside. The cold temperatures are just too dangerous to be outside for any length of time. Your parents may have plans to do something else fun inside for the evening instead. In such cold weather, you could easily lose your fingers and toes, and that's not a very nice trick on Halloween. So enjoy the treats you've received here at school instead of going out this evening. Perhaps enjoy Charlie Brown on television or play family games instead. Be sure to bundle up, because no one is leaving these doors without their winter weather apparel on their person."

Maeve listened and was very thankful the school was taking the harsh weather seriously. She'd hate to think of children getting stranded off the school bus on their way home for any length of time in this dangerous cold without their coats on.

Maeve scanned the crowd for her little cowboy, and soon she spotted him with his floppy brown hat on. *It must be a parent thing. I can look into any group and zone in on my own child almost instantly.*

Ben spotted her too, and as she stood there shivering, she motioned with her hand for him to come to her. He got up from his spot on the floor and waded through the other boys and girls dressed as everything from princesses to a creative slice of pepperoni pizza.

"Hi, Mom," he said, dragging his school backpack and coat behind him.

"You ready?"

He nodded.

"You heard the principal. Put on your coat and gloves."

Ben didn't protest this time since he saw several of his buddies also putting on their outerwear. "They canceled Halloween?" Ben asked quizzically, trying to make sense of what the principal was trying to convey.

"Sort of. It's way too cold, so it's not safe to be exposed outside right now. Let's hurry and get you in the car before the parking lot turns chaotic." She took her son by his gloved hand and led him outside. One step into the frigid air and the sharp cold took their breath away. Once Ben was strapped securely in his car seat, Maeve checked the rearview mirror again. The last thing she wanted to do was disappoint her son. He'd had far too much of that already in his young six years. And a parking lot crash wasn't a good idea either since she'd had a bad driver reputation to overcome since that morning.

His unruly brown mop was turned sideways as he contemplated the issues outside of the window. "Mom? If we don't do Halloween tonight, can we do it when the temperature gets warmer again?"

With an inner sigh of relief, she smiled. "Yes, of course, Ben. I'm certain a lot of other parents are considering the same thing. Sometimes Mother Nature makes you change even the best-laid plans. We'll cuddle up by the fire tonight and eat popcorn and watch movies. Does that sound like a good idea?"

"That's a very good idea, Mom," Ben said.


To PREVIEW and Purchase Surrender the Sun visit Amazon.

Printed in Poland
by Amazon Fulfillment
Poland Sp. z o.o., Wrocław

54473409R00116